ON THE EDGE OF INFINITY

BOOK 5

THE VAMPIRE NAVY SEAL SERIES

S.B. ALEXANDER

Cover designed by Hang Le
Cover copyright © 2021 by S.B. Alexander

On the Edge of Infinity
Book five: The Vampire Navy SEAL Series

First Edition: June 2017

E-book ISBN-13: 978-0-9989157-1-5
Paperback Print ISBN-13: 978-1-954888-00-5
Large Print ISBN – 13: 978-1-954888-02-9

WEBB

I paced the carpeted floor of Hollings's chamber. Jo and I had traveled to Boston to visit with her father. I didn't know what I was supposed to do with the state of our affairs. I couldn't get out of the military. My discharge papers had been denied. Steven Mason was in jail for murdering the Secretary of the Navy, and I was now in charge of a bag of shit. Yet, all I could think about was marrying Jo. I'd asked her to marry me, and she had said yes. But we couldn't tie the knot until we were free and clear of the hornets' nest we were in.

Jo was convinced that Edmund had killed the Secretary of the Navy and pinned the blame on Steven. It wasn't that I didn't believe her, because what she said was probably one hundred percent true. The pile of crap we were stuck in was figuring out how to prove Steven's innocence when the evidence the elders had against him seemed to prove his guilt without a question. They had the murder weapon—the dagger that slit the secretary's throat—with Steven's DNA on the blade. Why the dagger suddenly showed up months after the murder was also a burning question.

I shoved a hand through my hair, the back of which fell out of the leather strap.

Jo glided in, all five feet six inches of her. Her black hair was unbound and flowing like a smooth wave on a subtle breeze.

After two weeks of not being able to visit or talk with her father and working hard to help Dr. Vieira in the lab, Jo appeared tired and dazed. She hadn't been sleeping. I knew firsthand since I'd insisted on staying with her in the apartment that Steven called home on base. She hadn't protested, but I didn't think she would. I was the one having a hard time controlling my libido. I was the one who wanted to wait until we were married to make love. I wasn't sure I would be able to keep the promise that I'd made more for me than for her. Actually, I'd made the promise mostly to show her father that I was a gentleman. Still, with her long, silky legs and lavender scent, I could barely keep my hands off her, let alone sleep. But I would torture myself if it meant that she was happy and safe.

"How did they find the murder weapon? And where?" she asked for the millionth time.

I grabbed her by the shoulders. "The where doesn't matter. Your father's DNA is all over that dagger along with the secretary's."

Her nostrils flared. "The where *does* matter. It could lead us to the real murderer. I would bet the trail leads to Edmund. If you recall, around the time of the secretary's murder, Edmund and your sister, Kate, stole my dad's blood."

I flinched when she said Kate's name. Part of me had come to terms with her death. I flinched more when Jo looked away as she said my sister's name. She'd killed Kate in self-defense. I got that. I didn't blame Jo at all, but if the tables had been turned, I probably would have felt the same remorse if I'd killed her brother, Sam.

Jo waved a hand in front of my face. "Webb?" Then her nails grazed my unshaven jaw. "I'm sorry to bring up Kate. I'm also sorry that I was the one to end her life."

I met her silver gaze. Immediately, I relaxed. Jo had a way of calming me with her soft look and equally soft touch. She was my family now, and the earth could crumble, but we would get our happily ever after.

I sighed as I dragged my fingers down her cheek. "Please stop apologizing. Kate made her choice. You were protecting yourself."

She wrapped her arms around me. "I can't help but think that one day you'll hate me for what I've done."

I grasped her arms gently then eased back as I peered down at her. "Never, angel. I love you. You're my life now. Forever."

Her eyes bled from silver to violet, water pooling in them.

"We'll get through this," I whispered since I was getting choked up too.

She angled her head as the color of her eyes turned a dark violet. "My dad is innocent."

"I know he is. I recall that day vividly." I started pacing again in front of the large cherry credenza while Jo watched me. "Your dad met with the Secretary of the Navy that morning after we dropped you and Sam off at school. If you recall, that's the same day you killed Blake Turner. So your dad had to rush out of his meeting when I called him. When he left a room full of government officials, the secretary included, no one was dead. But the evidence is damning. Maybe we'll have luck with the coroner's report. That should show the time of death, which could prove your father's innocence."

She pursed her lips. "Not if Edmund bribed the coroner or threatened him. Or if he's bribing one of the elders. Maybe one of the elders is in on Edmund's plan to take out my father. Remember, Edmund wants to run the military. Again, he told me so two weeks ago when I was having a decent conversation with him." She ran her tongue across the tip of one of her fangs.

"Jo, please. You have to calm down." I had to calm down. I was as worked up as she was, not only because of her father's circumstances but because Edmund knew about his daughter, Abbey, and Steven had yet to divulge the whereabouts of Abbey and her mom, Rachel.

I couldn't protect them if I didn't know where they were.

Edmund wanted his daughter, and if I knew him—and I did—he wouldn't stop until he got Abbey. I couldn't blame him. After all, she was his daughter. The problem was that Rachel didn't want Abbey anywhere near Edmund. Steven and I didn't, either. Edmund would use his daughter as a lab rat, especially when he found out the little girl had supernatural powers at the age of four, which was unheard of in our world.

Jo darted over to Hollings's desk that sat in front of the window. "What I need is to get to Edmund. I need to find him and—"

"And what? He's not going to confess. He's not coming in to get locked up or put to his death if Victor has any say in this." Victor Costner was a ticking time bomb who wanted Edmund's head on a platter for injecting a new form of vampire serum into Victor's grandson, Matthew. "And let's not forget that Edmund wants Abbey."

She sifted through files on the desk. "I would stake my life on the fact that Edmund mailed the murder weapon to Hollings with a letter."

I hurried over to her as she threw one folder aside and dove into another. I caught her wrist. "Stop. Are you insane? If Hollings walks in, he'll throw you in a cell."

She shrugged out of my hold. "So?" She started opening drawers.

I grasped her arm and pulled her to me. She pushed me, but I was stronger.

She let out a soft growl. "I can't sit around and do nothing. I'm tired of Edmund screwing up our lives. I want him dead."

I glanced around, hoping the walls weren't thin. "Keep your voice down. If Edmund did show up dead somewhere, you would be the first one they'd implicate. Besides, if Edmund is responsible for the secretary's murder, then we need him alive."

She huffed as she relaxed in my arms.

I rested my chin on her head. "You know what you need?"

"You," she blurted out as she peered up at me. "I want you. I don't want to wait for our wedding night to consummate our love for each other. I'm dying here, Webb. I sleep with you every night, and the more we're together, the more I can't contain myself. I know you want me. I feel you every damn waking minute. I'm literally going to explode."

I grinned like an ass. She was so incredibly beautiful with her flushed cheeks and her eyes flashing from silver to violet.

She pouted. "Are you mocking me?"

I ushered her over to the window. The city skyline of Boston twinkled against the backdrop of the setting sun. The days were getting shorter as we entered November.

"I would never mock you. You're my angel. You do things to me that I've never experienced in my life. I want you so badly that it's hard with you rubbing against me night after night. But I want all the time in the world to show you how much I love you. And tonight, we'll start with a romantic night in Boston. No phones, no fights, and no biting on nails." I winked. "Just necks." I'd been wanting to do something I hadn't had the chance to do since I proposed, and tonight I was going to do it.

"Time is precious, Webb." Her voice was breathy. "Who knows if we'll be here tomorrow or an hour from now? If we wait for Edmund to come clean or die, we could be waiting a lifetime to get married."

I twisted her to face me, and I wasted no time capturing her lips in mine. "You're right. But I want to be the perfect gentleman."

She arched into me. "Screw being a gentleman." She wiggled her sweet hips into my groin. "See, you want me. It doesn't take much for you to react to my body. Please, just one night, then we can wait until we're married."

I chuckled as my fangs grazed her jaw down to her neck, where her pulse beat rapidly. The best thing about our relationship was the explosion of feelings that erupted when I bit her. Jo's blood did things to me, and the more blood I took, the stronger those things got. At first, I would get dizzy, high, and I would feel anything she felt. Anything she thought about, I got a glimpse of. But the more we drank from each other, the more we were connected, and the more my body craved her. She was right. Time was precious, and I didn't want to waste another minute without showing her how beautiful she was.

I was about to sink my fangs into her when I heard footsteps outside the door. An elder's chambers wasn't the place to show Jo how I felt, and I certainly needed to be the commander in charge in front of Hollings, not some horny vampire only after my boss's daughter.

In vampire speed, I had us both settled into the chairs in front of the desk.

Jo giggled as her rosy cheeks darkened. "It's not a crime to kiss me."

"It might be if I got out of control," I teased as the door opened.

Hollings strutted in, smoothing a hand over his thick dark hair. His wide black eyes were trained on me. "Doing something you're not supposed to?" He circled his desk as his gaze lingered too long on me.

Jo slowly slid her foot over to mine and kicked me. It took me a minute to realize the folders on Hollings's desk were scattered and not in a neat pile like they had been before Jo tackled the contents.

"Just spending time with my girl," I said. "Can we see Commander Mason now?"

He collected the out-of-place folders. "He's meeting with his attorney. They should be done momentarily. Before you head down, I wanted to talk to both of you." He folded his bulk into his chair. "Let's start with you, Jo. Tell me about Edmund. I understand you've had quality time with him. Has he opened up to you about anything?"

Jo sat back in the wooden armchair as she chewed on her bottom lip. "What exactly do you want to know?"

I opened up a telepathic connection to her. *Until we know who the mole is, don't tell him much.*

Hollings leaned forward with his elbows on his desk. "Other than building an army of vampires out of humans who don't carry the vampire gene, what else is he after?"

"Power. He wants my dad's job. Hence, why he's framing my dad."

"I don't disagree. Someone definitely wants your father out of the picture. But Edmund knows he could never command a SEAL team or step foot on a military base again."

She pinched her eyebrows together. "Why would he want something he can't have?"

"Maybe he thinks he can have it," Hollings said. "Maybe his plan is to kill you, your family, the elders, the SEAL team—"

"Or maybe Edmund has someone working on the inside," I said. "So he knows he'll get what he wants."

"You mean someone on the council of elders?" Hollings asked.

I rubbed the stubble on my chin. "Someone who can make the decision or at least be Edmund's cheerleader. Edmund can't commandeer an entire vampire community without help. And he can't rule the military without someone on the inside. Which is probably why he killed the Secretary of the Navy. He knew the secretary would never appoint him to any position."

The puzzle pieces were coming together. Edmund had to have someone on the council in his court or on the team of humans within the government. He needed someone who knew about vampires and who could make those high-level decisions. But as I studied Hollings, I didn't get the sense he was that person, at least not with the curious expression on his face. If I had hit a nerve, then I would've gotten a different reaction.

Hollings tapped his forefinger on his lips. "Interesting observation, Lieutenant."

"Is Webb right?" Jo blurted out.

Hollings shook his head. "I don't know."

"The mole could be you," Jo said.

Hollings narrowed his eyes. "Jo, be careful."

Jo slid her butt to the edge of her seat. "With all due respect, I trust no one. Plus, it's odd that you were appointed to the elder position not that long ago, and now the murder weapon shows up."

"Jo," I warned. Elders had free rein to punish someone as they saw fit.

She jumped up. "No, Webb. I'm tired of always looking over my shoulder, of worrying if Edmund is going to kidnap me, or what surprise he's going to dish out next. We know he's working with someone within the vampire government. Or maybe he's working with more than one person. But we have to attack this like everyone is a suspect."

I chuckled when I should have been agreeing with her. But she was acting as though she was a seasoned detective, and I was dumbfounded at her strategic thinking.

Hollings grinned too.

She stomped her foot, her eyes flashing vampire. "Stop mocking me. Both of you."

"Jo," Hollings said. "You raise all good points. And while you might not believe me, I'm not the mole. I do, however, agree that a mole within our organization, whether in my circle or the SEAL's circle, does exist. But we have to work together to bring Edmund down once and for all."

Her eyes went wide. "Really?" She sat back down.

Hollings interlocked his fingers. "Yes. Edmund has wreaked havoc since his departure from the military. The elders are tired and quite frustrated with covering up his dirty work. Those within the human government who don't know about vampires are starting to question things. Their superiors are not going to be able to keep the lid on our world much longer. We thought with Bruno dead, we could breathe a little. But with dead human bodies showing up in alleys and dumpsters in the last two weeks, it's just a matter of time before humans find out about our existence. With the lab explosion on the Indian reservation, the same place Edmund was holding you, the media and government are wondering why the dead bodies found at the scene have canines that rival wolves. We can't let the public know about us. We have to put a stop to all this, which is why you're here. I need your help, Jo."

My gut told me I wasn't about to like his next statement.

Hollings sat back. "The elders have agreed that we need someone on the inside of Edmund's operation. Someone who can gain Edmund's trust. I feel that person is you, Jo."

Jo choked then laughed. "Me?"

"No way," I blurted out. "She almost got killed the last time she was with Edmund. And what if one of the other elders is the mole? They'll tell Edmund immediately. Sir, let me do my job. You want Edmund's operation shut down? Then let me handle this. My team and I will do everything we can to bring him in."

Hollings rose. "Steven believes the only match to take out Edmund is Jo."

"What?" Jo and I asked at the same time.

Hollings tucked a hand into his pants pocket. "Go down and chat with your father. I need to rethink my strategy. Then we can talk again when I get back from my business trip in a couple of days."

His strategy wasn't worth shit. My team and I had come up with the strategy to take out an enemy, not an elder.

"What about my dad?" Jo bounced her knee. "He's innocent."

"Until we can put all the pieces of the puzzle together on the secretary's murder, we can't let your father out of jail," Hollings said. "Besides, right now, the top echelons within the human government are content, knowing we have a suspect."

I stood and held out my hand to Jo, cursing under my breath that Hollings thought he could run the show. Maybe he could with Steven in command, but not with me. Maybe the blessing in disguise was that Steven was out of the picture for now. That way, I could get shit done.

2

———

JO

As soon as Webb and I were in the elevator, I tightened my shoulders, ready to argue with him over why I had mouthed off to an elder. Instead of questioning my actions, he checked his phone.

I relaxed as the elevator traveled down to the second floor. "Are you really going to bring Edmund in alive?"

He lifted his cobalt-blue gaze. My stomach fluttered.

"I didn't promise I would. I said I would do everything I could."

"I have to be honest. I had every intention of trying to find a way to work for Edmund behind your back, but I decided last night that wouldn't be a smart move. And if I did work for Edmund, he would only use me or kill me, and he would never trust me."

Webb snagged me to him. At the moment, I had this love/hate relationship with the handsome vampire. Or I should say I had more of a frustrated feeling that made me want to scream at him at the top of my lungs. I loved being close to him, kissing him, and doing so much more, but I wanted to take our relationship to the next level. He had some hang-up about waiting until we were married.

He tipped up my chin. "Let's talk to your father before we make any decisions." He leaned down and kissed me lightly on the lips. "And thank you for being honest."

I didn't want our relationship to be based on lies, and if we were going to capture or kill Edmund, we had to do it as a team. Edmund always had something up his sleeve, and his powers were getting stronger. Not only that, but if Edmund could read minds, I had to practice blocking him. I'd gotten better at keeping my father out of my head, but my dad wasn't the enemy, and Edmund could use tactics to get in my head. I didn't know what those tactics were, but I had to be prepared.

"Together, we're stronger. Our minds are in sync. Well, on some topics, they're in sync." I gritted my teeth, not only because of Edmund but because I wanted to climb up Webb's body and do sexy things to him that I'd only dreamed about.

His eyes flashed to vampire black. "Just think how beautiful making love will be when we have all the time in the world."

I poked a finger in his chest. "And what if we don't make it to our wedding?"

He cupped my face. "We will not die or fail in our mission to shut Edmund down."

"You know this how?" I wanted to believe him, although I hadn't had any dreams to tell me otherwise like I'd had when I dreamt that Webb's mission to Alaska would fail.

"For the first time in my life, I have someone who I'm deeply in love with, and I will not let anyone or anything take you away from me. Besides, you just said we're stronger together."

Dad, Sam, and Webb wanted to protect me, and while I loved them for that, I wasn't sitting on the sidelines. "Then promise me one thing. I'm your equal in this fight. We make decisions together."

The elevator bell dinged before the door slid open.

He kissed me on the lips. "You have my promise."

I could have read his mind to be sure he was telling me the truth unless he'd taken that magic potion that Ms. Costner had whipped up to block anyone from his thoughts. I decided against it. I had to trust him.

The elevator was about to close. I didn't move as a thought hit me. I could get Ms. Costner to whip up a batch for me. That way, Edmund couldn't read my mind.

Webb grabbed the door then took my hand. "What is it?"

"I just realized that the potion Ms. Costner made for you to block anyone from reading your mind would help me if we decided to send me in to work for Edmund."

He cocked an eyebrow. "Brilliant."

I squared my shoulders, feeling quite sated that I'd come up with a great idea.

We wound our way down the cold hallway to the guardian who was standing at attention outside the room in which my dad was being held. Webb and I came to a halt, while the vampire with beady brown eyes and a goatee waved a wand over me then Webb. Once we were cleared, he knocked twice before someone on the inside opened the heavy door.

We were met by another guardian who, like the one outside, was dressed in a dark business suit. The majority of the guardians that worked for the elders were always dressed in suits rather than police-like uniforms.

The small, claustrophobic room had no windows, but it did have a table and two chairs, which were occupied by my dad and his attorney, Mr. Rose.

My dad rushed over and threw his arms around me. "Pumpkin, I've missed you."

I squeezed him as hard as I could. I'd been in foster care most of my life, so when my dad found Sam and me, our father-daughter relationship had been tense. Since then, we'd come a long way, and I loved him dearly.

He brushed my hair off my shoulder. "You look tired."

"I'm okay," I said. "You're the one who looks like hell."

Dad's black hair was rather long and oily, and black circles marred the underside of his dull green eyes.

"Have you had blood recently?" I quickly glanced at Webb, who had the same concerned look that I probably had.

"We'll remedy that," Mr. Rose said on my left.

I shifted my gaze to my best friend's dad, who didn't look as haggard as he had when he worked on my case. Then again, my court trial had been several months ago, and Mr. Rose's problems of owing a vampire a ton of money had been settled thanks to my dad.

Mr. Rose raked his brown gaze over my face. "It's good to see you. Darcy misses you."

I missed her too. "As much as I would like to see her, I better not for now. But do tell her she will be my maid of honor." I beamed as I batted my eyelashes at Webb.

Mr. Rose's eyes went wide as he regarded Webb then me. "Congratulations. When is the big day?"

"We're not sure yet," Webb said. "We've got problems to deal with at the moment."

Mr. Rose stuffed his belongings into his briefcase. "Steven, let's resume our discussion tomorrow. Jo. Webb. It was good to see you." With his briefcase in hand, he walked out.

"Snyder, give us a few minutes," Dad said to the guard.

The sharply dressed vampire studied Dad. I scratched my head as to why the guardian was even in the room. With no windows and one exit, which Snyder was protecting, Dad couldn't escape unless he could teleport, and no vampire in our world had that ability.

Without a word, Snyder removed himself, closing the door with a soft click.

Dad sat down, while Webb held out the other chair for me. Then he anchored himself to a spot on the wall off to my right.

"So, talk to me," Dad said. "Tell me what's going on back on base."

"First, Dad, did you tell Hollings that I was the only one who could take out Edmund?"

Dad closed his eyes for a second. "I didn't say that. What I said was that Edmund might open up to you again, although it will take more than one person to bring Edmund down. The bigger questions to consider are—how is he gaining more supernatural powers? How is he able to read minds? Has my brother, Patrick, developed some type of concoction that is making Edmund's powers stronger? No other vampires have had the power our family has had."

I gnawed on my lip. "And why didn't he or I die when we were both stabbed in the heart with a cobalt dagger?" That one question had been plaguing me since our showdown at the funeral home a couple of weeks ago. I'd asked Dr. Vieira, but his conclusion had been that the dagger missed our hearts.

Dad rested his elbows on the table. "I agree with Dr. Vieira. Regardless, we need to infiltrate Edmund's organization. We need to shut him down. We need to destroy all the research that Patrick has done. We cannot let anyone get their hands on that data. Then we can focus on killing Edmund."

"What about getting you out of jail?" I asked.

"Don't worry about me, pumpkin. Mr. Rose is a good lawyer. He'll gather all the evidence and legal documents and do his job just as well on my case as he did on your murder trial. In the meantime, Webb, I want you and your team to focus on Edmund. Find him. Put out feelers. Check with our military sources in Alaska. The elders want Edmund alive to prosecute him, but we may have a bigger problem." Dad stared at Webb, who had an unreadable mask on his face.

"What could be bigger than Edmund?" I asked as the room dropped into dead silence. Dad and Webb had to be speaking telepathically.

Several minutes ticked by until Webb pushed off the wall and began pacing. "You've got to be kidding me."

"Under no circumstances can we let any of that happen," Dad said.

"Care to let me in?" I knew they wouldn't if Dad found it necessary to speak telepathically.

Webb's nostrils flared. "Later."

"How's Matthew Costner and the other human we rescued from Edmund two weeks ago?" Dad changed his staunch demeanor as though someone had flipped a switch.

I shrugged. "The human isn't awake yet. Dr. Vieira says he has a pulse, but it might be a while before the boy comes out of the comatose state. As for Matthew, he's a healthy vampire. He can even go outside in the sun."

Dad scrubbed a hand over his unshaven jaw. "I can't say I'm surprised with Matthew. After all, he comes from a long line of vampires."

"But he doesn't carry the vampire gene," I added. Dr. Vieira had once explained that natural-born vampires were produced by a male vampire and a human female who had Vel-negative blood type, which meant that Matthew's father wasn't a vampire.

"No, but again, his maternal side is made up of all vampires," Webb chimed in.

"And how is Ben?" Dad asked.

Dad had taken a liking to Ben, finally.

Webb settled back against the wall. "Ben is learning to deal with his half human and half vampire state. He'll be a good asset to the SEAL team in the future."

I smiled. Ben's dream had always been to become a Navy SEAL, although not as a mixed breed, which was what Dr. Vieira had dubbed Ben.

"What about Mr. Jackson?" Dad asked. "Has Ben contacted his father?"

Webb shook his head. "We're not there yet. Ben still has issues controlling the change in his eye color. However, he has talked to his father on the phone to let him know that he joined the military and that he'll be able to come home when boot camp is over."

That wasn't a total lie. Webb and his team along with my

brother, Sam, had been training Ben on all things military and vampire.

"So, Dad, do you think I should work for Edmund?" I wanted to do everything and anything to stop Edmund from succeeding, but we hadn't been successful in any of our missions to thwart him. Even the dagger Sam had driven through his heart hadn't killed him. I wasn't sure I could or would be able to wipe Edmund off the face of the planet.

Dad rubbed his chin. "I think that decision is up to you and Webb. I know Webb will come up with a solid plan. I also know we need to snuff out the mole. Whoever he or she is has been giving Edmund information, which is why he is always one step ahead of us." Dad glanced at Webb. "Don't tell anyone what your plans are, not even the elders. Select a handful of SEALs and no one else. Having said all that, I do want you to consider Jonah to be one of your team members."

Webb opened his mouth.

Dad held up his hand. "Hear me out. Jonah has always been Edmund's right-hand man. While you were detained in Alaska, Tripp was trying to get him on our side."

I'd forgotten all about Jonah. Webb had captured him at one of the SEALs' raids, and as far as I knew, Jonah had been in the base prison.

"We transferred Jonah to this facility I'm in a month ago," Dad said. "I've been chatting with him for the last two weeks."

"Why would he work for us?" Webb asked.

Dad's eyes lit up. "Because he learned recently that Edmund killed a human girl Jonah was in love with."

"How did Jonah find out?" Webb asked. "Does he have contact with Edmund?"

"He overheard Hollings and I talking the other night about a list of humans who have shown up dead. Since then, I was able to not only chat with him, but read his mind. I think we could put him to good use."

"Did you find anything in his head about Edmund killing the Secretary of the Navy?" I asked. If Jonah was Edmund's bitch, then he should know if Edmund murdered the secretary.

"He wasn't with Edmund that night," Dad said. "But my brother was."

Webb shook his head. "Patrick won't testify."

Snyder came in. "Commander, it's time to go back to your cell."

Dad pushed to his feet. "I agree about Patrick. But one step at a time. Think about what we talked about. Start planning. The sooner we get Edmund out of the picture, the sooner we can get on with our lives."

I rose. "We need to get you out first."

Dad skirted the table and pulled me in for a hug. "I told you not to worry."

Tears pricked my eyes. "I do worry. I want you to walk me down the aisle. I want you in my life."

He rubbed a hand down my back. "I love you too. Look, I want you and Webb to do whatever it takes to stop Edmund's operation."

And I wanted the same thing, but I also wanted to clear my dad of the murder charge. I had to somehow coax Edmund into a confession or maybe plead with my uncle Patrick to help his own brother.

3

WEBB

The lights in the hotel lobby were too bright for me. I felt as though I was on display at some auction. I did what I always did when entering a room—I checked for exits, I opened up my hearing and listened to conversations of people milling around, I swept the room, far and wide, quickly assessing each person who was either lounging in the sitting area, standing in line in front of us at the check-in counter, and those who were close by in the restaurant. As a SEAL, I was taught that no place was safe, and trust was hard to come by. Jo hovered close to me, searching the lobby too. I took comfort in knowing that she didn't take anything for granted when she walked into an unknown place.

I snaked my arm around her waist. "We're good."

She sighed. "I know, but I had to be sure. I get the feeling we're being watched."

"You should always have that feeling in a foreign place, no matter if you know the area or not."

"When are you going to tell me what my dad told you?"

"When the time is right." I wasn't about to divulge anything in a hotel lobby, and even then, I was contemplating whether to tell her at all. I could very well open a telepathic connection. However, Steven had warned me to keep the information close to my vest. Not only that, but if Jo happened to meet up with Edmund, and he did have mind-reading capabilities, I couldn't risk her knowing anything about the CIA and their plan to extract all Patrick's research so they could build super soldiers for their military.

"Tonight, we don't talk shop. Tonight is about you and me."

Her silver eyes glistened as a smidgeon of violet shone through.

"Easy, angel. The last time you switched eye color in public, the press took pictures." We couldn't afford drawing attention from the media or anyone else.

Her hand slid up my chest as we waited in line to check in. "What's on the agenda, then?"

Spending the night in a hotel was probably a bad idea since Jo was getting more frustrated by the day with me ignoring her advances, and I was a moron for torturing myself in the process as well. But I couldn't care less how much I drove myself crazy as long as Jo was at my side. Sure, she could handle herself, but as she'd said, we were stronger together, and we were. I couldn't explain why I had added strength with her near me. It was as though I was invincible. I suspected her blood had something to do with it. I made a mental note to consult with Dr. Vieira.

"After we check in, we're going shopping," I said.

She snorted. "You? Shopping? The last time we shopped was at a Target in Maine, and if I recall, you were antsy to get out of the store."

We shuffled forward when the businessman in front of us stepped up to the counter.

"You'll like what's in store," I whispered. "And please don't read my mind. I want this to be a surprise." I wished I had some of the mind-blocking potion from Alia Costner, but my only supply was at my house in Maine.

"We need to talk with Alia soon," Jo said.

The businessman walked by us as Jo and I stepped up to the

pretty brunette behind the counter. I pulled out my wallet and handed her my credit card.

"Do you have a reservation?" the clerk asked.

"Yes. Under London."

The clerk smiled, her dark gaze lingering too long on me. Before Jo tensed up too much, the clerk's fingers tapped on the keyboard.

I squeezed Jo tightly against me then opened up a telepathic connection. *You can't keep getting jealous every time a lady looks at me.*

She giggled. *Says the possessive vampire.*

"Well, Mr. and Mrs. London, we have your suite ready for you. And as you instructed, Mr. London, the garment bags are in the bedroom closet. Your car should arrive within the hour. I'll ring the room when the driver gets here." She handed my credit card back to me along with a room key.

I collected the cards. "Thank you, Ms. Bliss."

We made our way through the bright lobby, past guests who were lounging on couches and deeply immersed in their mobile devices.

Jo was beaming from ear to ear. "Mr. And Mrs., huh? That has a nice ring to it."

I had also warmed at the sound of Mr. and Mrs. London.

My phone rang as Jo stabbed the up arrow for the elevator.

"Hey, George," I said into my phone.

"I wanted to check in. I have some news on Edmund. You know that vampire Howell, who got burned up in the lab explosion? He's been in contact with his uncle."

I growled. The last thing I needed was any grief from Howell, even though Olivia and I had saved his life. "Well, he can't be working for Bruno since Bruno is dead. But I sense you're about to tell me Howell is working for Edmund again."

The elevator dinged, but I pulled Jo away and found a quiet corner near the restrooms.

"No, he's not. But he wants to repay you for saving his life. He wants to work for you. He feels he can get back into Edmund's organization and help in some way."

That was an interesting thought. Since Howell had worked for Edmund, he might have an easier time getting inside than us. "Let me think on it. Don't say anything to his uncle until I make my decision."

"Very well," George said. "Are you at the hotel yet?"

"Jo and I just arrived. I'll call you soon." Then I hung up.

Jo and I found our way up to the suite on the top floor of the Waldorf. Once inside the luxury suite that was bigger than the first floor of my house in Maine, I snagged Jo to me.

"You and I will have a night to remember." Before she could speak, I shoved my tongue in her mouth, something I'd been dying to do all day. I also didn't want her to protest, ask too many questions, or read my mind—the latter being difficult. I couldn't spoil the surprise. So as much as the visions of her and me naked tortured the fuck out of me, I had to distract her. It was the only way to keep her from getting in my head.

She mewled softly, and instantly my groin reacted. Images of me kissing my way down her naked body filled my head. All of a sudden, my hands were everywhere on her body, ripping her clothes off before carrying her into the bedroom.

With our lips fused together, she giggled on the way. When she was completely naked, lying on the bed with her stark black hair fanned out and wild, her cheeks rosy, and her nipples standing at attention, I almost fell to my knees. Instead, I climbed on top of her, careful not to touch her until I lowered my head and locked my eyes with hers. She batted those long lashes I so loved, then I captured a nipple into my mouth. She arched into me, noises falling from her beautiful lips. I abandoned one nipple to play with the other, sucking, tasting, teasing as I dropped into a deep lustful world where no sounds existed and no light shone in. The darkness around us was magical as I continued my assault on her satin-smooth skin. I kissed my way down her abs as I shaped her curves with one hand. She spewed soft groans, her body writhing, her hands pulling on my hair.

When I reached the apex of her legs, I lifted my head. Words couldn't describe how beautiful she was. Her silver eyes glowed to a deep violet as her fangs dropped. Before I could make my next move, I was on my back and she was on top of me.

I grinned, showing my own fangs. The beauty of our vampire heritage was our strength, and I got harder just thinking about how she could give me a run for my money.

My phone rang, but the trilling and annoying sound didn't stop Jo from tearing off my shirt. Her nails scored my bare chest, and I watched in quiet fascination how she took in every inch of me as though she was trying to memorize each muscle, dip, and valley on my upper torso.

The ringing stopped then restarted.

I grasped her hips. "Angel, I need to answer my phone. Someone needs me."

She flopped on the bed, huffing. "I need you."

I got up with an erection harder than a diamond. But I was getting used to the pain in my groin. I had willpower, but when it came to Jo, my restraint was waning at a rapid rate.

The ringing stopped again as I pulled my phone out of my cargo pants. "Why don't you get dressed? Your garment bag is in the closet." I stalked out into the living room and over to the window. Lights twinkled from the building across the street.

Before I had a chance to check who had called, the phone lit up once again. "What is it, Tripp?"

"Lieutenant." Tripp's voice sounded concerned, which was unusual for him or any SEAL. "The human that came in with Matthew Costner didn't make it."

"I know you didn't make an urgent phone call to tell me that."

"The human is the Secretary of the Navy's son."

I pinched the bridge of my nose. "Are you certain?"

"Yep, DNA confirms that the human is Cory Andrews, age twenty-eight, born to Owen and Yvonne Andrews."

I grabbed the back of my neck. "How come we haven't heard of Cory's disappearance? I would've thought that if he was missing, it would've been all over the news."

"Not unless the government is keeping his disappearance under wraps," Tripp said. "I wanted you to know in case you're still with the commander."

"I'm not. Find out more about Cory. Where was the last place he was seen? Who was he with? But do it discreetly. What I mean is don't engage anyone in the control room. We still don't know who the mole is. By the way, who else knows about this?"

Jo's lavender scent filled the room before I caught a reflection of her in the window. I slowly turned as Tripp said something in my ear. But all I could focus on was the way the silver dress clung to Jo's body, accentuating her supple breasts and sleek curves.

"Lieutenant, are you there?" Tripp kept asking.

I shook off the effects that Jo was having on my brain. "Sorry. Please repeat."

Jo's long bare legs carried her over to me. "What's going on?"

I held up my finger.

"The only ones that know about this are Dr. Vieira, Dr. Case, Olivia, and me," Tripp said. "When are you returning to base?"

"Jo and I will be there in the morning," I said then hung up.

She smoothed her hand down the silky knee-length dress before she twirled around, showing me how the fabric dipped in a V down to her lower back.

I held in a growl.

"What do you think? Did you pick this out for me?"

I couldn't take the credit. "George did." I wasn't a shopper in the least. "I did have a say in the color, though." I always imagined her dressed in the color silver to bring out her eyes, even when they were violet or black.

"Well, I love it. And the silky fabric feels wonderful against my body."

I traced a finger over the swell of her breasts. "I will feel better against your body."

She eased back. "Tease. Get dressed, or else I will force you to make love to me against your wishes, gentleman London."

I didn't doubt that she could make me do whatever she wanted. "If you can break my willpower," I said playfully as I blew past her and into the bedroom.

She followed me in. "I'm very close to breaking you." Her tone was so serious.

I chuckled. Thankfully, the driver was due to be there shortly. I couldn't miss the small window I had to take her to the place I'd been planning for the last week.

"What did Tripp want?" she asked.

I changed into the suit that George had gotten for me. "The human we brought in with Matthew died. And that human was none other than the Secretary of the Navy's son."

"Really?" She slipped her feet into the gray pumps that George had also bought for her. "Then doesn't that say that Edmund had something to do with both of their deaths?"

"For the son, yes. For the father, no. But Mr. Rose can argue otherwise. Right now, we can't do much."

The phone beside the bed rang. I finished buttoning my shirt then answered. "Hello."

"Mr. London, your driver is here in the lobby," the clerk said.

"We'll be down in five minutes." I hung up.

Jo grabbed a black fabric wrap and covered her bare shoulders. After one last quick kiss on her lips, we headed out.

The driver wound through the busy streets of Boston until he double-parked in front of a building that had no signs and no lights.

"We've dressed up to come to an abandoned building for dinner?" Jo asked.

I kept my expression as blank as I could while my insides were doing some kind of salsa dancing. I didn't doubt that George had set up something spectacular based on the list I'd given him. Regardless, I began to sweat.

The driver got out then circled around to the passenger side and opened the back door. I slipped out first before nodding at the human man, who seemed nervous as he scanned the streets.

"Don't worry," I said to him. "The neighborhood is safe." From what George had told me, the abandoned-looking brick buildings were home to a community of vampires who didn't like living among the dense neighborhoods in Boston that were filled with humans. "Once we're inside, find a coffee shop nearby. I'll call you when we're ready to leave."

Jo scooted to the edge of the seat before she took my clammy hand. I kept reciting daggers, swords, and guns as she wrapped her arm around mine.

"You're trying to keep me out of your mind," she said with a huge smile.

We walked up to the dull-green door and rang the bell. As we waited, my heart beat like a rocket on liftoff.

A short, skinny vampire answered. "Mr. London?" He waved us in. "I'm Deacon. I'll be your host this evening."

Jo stayed tethered to me, and I continued to think of weapons as we followed Deacon down a long, narrow, darkened hall until we reached the arched doorway at the very end.

"Here you go, Mr. London." Deacon handed me a blindfold. "I'll meet you inside." He disappeared.

With our vampire vision, it wasn't hard to see that Deacon had handed me a red piece of cloth. I prayed Jo couldn't see into the darkened room beyond the archway.

"What's that for?" Jo's tone was shaky as she let go of me.

"Do you trust me?" I asked.

"Of course." Her eyes flashed vampire. "But you're kind of scaring me."

"I promise what's about to happen will be something you'll

remember for the rest of your life." And mine. I couldn't wait to see her expression when I took off the blindfold. "Close your eyes."

She obeyed, her chest rising and falling, her pulse beating rapidly in my ears.

I tied the soft fabric around her eyes, careful not to touch her too long in the event she did dip into my mind while I was thinking of what waited beyond the doorway. After the blindfold was secure, I turned her so that she was facing the open archway. "I want you to walk straight ahead. I'll be right behind you."

Her breathing became heavy as she tentatively took the first step.

"It's okay. The floor is level, and there isn't anything in your way."

She laughed, albeit nervously. "I never took you for a kinky vampire."

Now it was my turn to laugh. But I wasn't about to think of sex. That would come after the wedding. Tonight was about starting our lives together. I wanted to give Jo the world and everything she ever wanted. She deserved happiness even if it was just for the moment, and I wanted to bask in her excitement when I took off that blindfold.

She walked slowly, and the lights overhead came on, a soft glow spraying down from the high ceilings above. Deacon had donned a white pair of gloves and was standing off to my left with his hands cupped in front of him. I smiled his way, nodding.

He couldn't help but return the gesture. Anyone about to witness what was about to happen had to smile because the moment that Jo realized what surrounded her would be epic.

"Jo," I said softly. "Stop." I inched up so I was standing in front of her. "I'm going to take off the blindfold now. But before I do, I want you to know a couple of things." My pulse sprinted in time with hers. "I am deeply and hopelessly in love with you. You make my world brighter, and I want to spend forever with you."

"Why do you sound like there's a *but* coming?" Her tone was taut.

I slowly untied the blindfold. "What I'm trying to say is tonight is the beginning of our lives together." I dropped the red piece of fabric.

She blinked several times before she glanced around the room. Her eyes shuddered from silver to violet then back several times as her mouth hung open.

I held my breath, waiting for her to say something. She twirled, mesmerized by the six glass cases that were set up in a U-shape around us. She flicked her gaze to me, tears idling on the rim of her lashes.

"The choice is yours, angel," I said in her ear. Then I kissed her lightly on the neck. "Go. Have fun."

Her heels clicked on the wood floor as she ambled up to the glass case opposite the arched doorway. Deacon jumped into action and positioned himself behind the counter full of diamonds of all shapes and sizes. Each glass case housed gold, silver, and twinkling stones.

"Does one catch your eye?" Deacon asked, his high forehead shining.

Jo turned toward me, waving her hand around. "Webb, this is too much. I don't need diamonds."

I sauntered up to her. "Maybe not, but I'm a traditional guy, and I want you to wear an engagement ring. I proposed but not properly."

She placed a trembling hand on my chest. "But I have you, and that's all I need."

I wrapped my fingers around her small wrist then brought her hand up to my lips and kissed her palm. "Please pick out one for me. I want to see a diamond on your finger."

Her lashes swept down, and a tear fell. "I don't want anything big or fancy, just simple."

"I have the perfect ring," Deacon said excitedly as he hurried over to a case that sat close to the entrance. He returned with a felt-lined tray that held a ring in the center. The square diamond was about a carat in weight with small amethyst stones set in the platinum band on each side of the diamond.

Jo's eyes popped out of her head as she stared at the ring.

"Ms. Mason," Deacon said. "You have your choice of any one of the two hundred rings we have in this room. So please look around. I just thought this one-point-five-carat diamond would be simple yet elegant on your finger. Plus, the amethyst stones will look exquisite on you with your eye color."

Her violet eyes were on display at the moment, and I had to agree that the design and setting were both simple yet beautiful, just like my fiancée.

I picked up the ring. "Let's try it on for size." I got down on one knee.

Tears flowed down Jo's cheeks as her hands trembled.

With the ring in between my shaky fingers, I glanced up at her. "Jo Mason, will you do me the honor of being by my side for eternity?"

She held out her left hand. "Eternity and beyond."

"That's a yes?" It wasn't that I doubted her answer, I just had to hear the simple word.

"Yes!" she shouted.

I slipped the ring on her finger before she tackled me to the warehouse floor, peppering kisses all over my face.

Deacon chuckled. "I guess she likes the ring?"

I managed to get us on our feet.

She stared at the diamond. "I absolutely love it." Then she set her gaze on Deacon. "You must know a woman's taste as soon as she walks through the door."

"I have been doing this for over a hundred years," he said. "But I'll leave you two alone for a few minutes while I get the paperwork." Deacon's heavy footsteps faded as he walked away.

I wasted no time in sealing our official engagement with a long, slow, body-humming kiss.

4

JO

I practically glided down the hall alongside Webb on our way to see Dr. Vieira. As much as our lives were in turmoil, I felt nothing could stop me from smiling today, or at least I wasn't about to let anything stop me from basking in my state of bliss. From Boston back to the base, I stared at the shiny stone on my finger. Last night with Webb had been amazing. After he'd officially proposed, we had a small quiet dinner at a quaint Italian restaurant in Boston. We chatted about the wedding mostly. After he'd given me the ring, I didn't want to ask or discuss anything that had to do with Edmund, my dad, vampires, or enemies.

Fast-forward fifteen hours, and I still didn't want to talk about our problems. On the drive back to the base, Webb had spoken to Tripp, but I ignored the conversation. I wanted to replay last night when he'd surprised me with a room full of expensive rings and when he'd said he wanted to get married on the beach outside his home in Maine. I didn't care where we tied the knot as long as our lives were free of Edmund.

Before we went into the lab, Webb kissed my temple. "Why don't you find your brother while I talk with Dr. Vieira?"

I wasn't ready to leave his side, although I did want to show Sam my ring. "I would like to see where Dr. Vieira is on the antidote." That wasn't a lie. I'd helped Dr. Vieira and Dr. Case with the testing of varying solutions on rats, and I was curious if they'd found the right mixture that would shield us for a longer period of time against the effects of the sedative bullets that Edmund used as his weapon of choice on us vampires.

However, I would have given anything to snuggle up to Webb like I had last night when the world was quiet, serene, and calming. No, he hadn't budged on his decision to wait before making love to me, and I hadn't pushed. I had to respect his wishes, and I knew that when we were finally married, he would not deny my requests any longer.

Webb smiled at me as though he knew what I was thinking. Maybe he did. He had been drinking from me, and when he did, he could always read my thoughts. But that was only when my blood was coursing through his system. Surely, he couldn't now.

"Can you read my mind?" I asked as he opened the double doors to the lab.

He cocked an eyebrow, but before he could respond, glass shattered. We both ran in, ready to fight.

"It's okay," Dr. Vieira said from somewhere in the room.

Then human blood scented the air. My fangs shot out as did Webb's. We both ran past the lab benches, desks, and computers until we found Dr. Vieira and Dr. Case picking up pieces of a broken beaker.

"My fault." Dr. Vieira's gold-rimmed glasses sat low on his nose. "Leroy, clean yourself up."

Dr. Case's warm brown eyes swam with fear. I couldn't blame him since he had three vampires surrounding him.

Webb grasped my arm, almost pulling me back. But I was used to the smell of human blood. Dr. Case had cut himself a couple of times while I'd helped out in the lab.

He jumped up then over to the sink where he ran water over his finger.

I darted over and retrieved the first aid kit from the cabinet above him while Webb helped Dr. Vieira.

"You're afraid," I said to Dr. Case. "How many times do we have to tell you we won't attack?"

"Every time," he said.

I helped him with the Band-Aid.

Once his cut was covered and the smell of human fear subsided, Dr. Case sauntered back to his spot on the bench in front of the microscope.

"Have you been able to tweak the antidote so that it works on us longer and reacts quicker?" I asked, following him.

Dr. Case looked into the microscope. "Not yet. But we're close."

Webb dipped his head into the fridge then emerged with three bottles of blood. I took one as a precaution, even though I wouldn't sink my fangs into Dr. Case. The blood coated my throat as I climbed onto a stool across from Dr. Case.

Webb sidled up to me, while Dr. Vieira washed his hands.

"What can I do for you, Webb?" Dr. Vieira asked as he walked over to stand beside Dr. Case.

"I wanted to chat with you in private if you have a minute," Webb said.

Dr. Case pulled away from the microscope, raking a hand through his hair. "Webb, before you left on your mission to Alaska, you made me a deal. I would decode the thumb drive you confiscated from your raid on Edmund's mansion, and in exchange, you would tell me who killed my sister, Ella. I know you've been gone for three months, but it's time we settle that deal. As a human, I can't be working around vampires."

I couldn't blame the doctor for feeling that way. Webb drank his blood as he considered Dr. Case. "Why haven't you left? Honestly, Commander Mason could've approved your request. After all, it's my understanding that you held up your end of the bargain."

"I approached the commander, and he wouldn't tell me who killed Ella. He said that was a deal that you and I made. And he wasn't getting involved. But he would let me leave on my own accord."

"Why did you decide to stay?" I asked. Up until now I'd never questioned Dr. Case's time there, and honestly, I'd forgotten all about the deal he made with Webb.

Dr. Case kept his gaze on Webb. "It's time you hold up your end and tell me who killed my sister."

Webb set down his empty bottle. "What will you do when I tell you?"

"Kill the bastard whether human or vampire."

Webb harrumphed. "You don't stand a chance if the person is a vampire."

Dr. Case swallowed hard, the sound reverberating in my ears. "As one of few humans who know vampires exist, I know how to kill your kind."

Webb's nostrils flared. "That may be, but with the fear oozing off you, you would be dead in a minute if you tried to kill a vampire."

Dr. Case straightened. "Why won't anyone tell me who killed my sister?"

Webb slammed a hand down on the bench. I flinched, Dr. Vieira jumped, and the blood drained from Dr. Case's face. In fact, his scent smelled of horrid fear.

"Let's recap your actions." Webb's voice sounded deadly. "First, you jump on the bandwagon with Patrick Mason and Edmund Rain to conspire to kill Jo and Sam when they were human. Then you help kidnap Sam, again when he was human. Oh, and you closed Jo in a coffin and left her to die. I could call the human police and see if they'll bring you up on charges for attempted murder."

"All that happened several months ago. You couldn't prove it. Besides, the police wouldn't believe you," he said very softly but firmly.

Webb's fangs shot out. "Don't test me, Case. And let's not forget Dr. Vieira and Commander Mason saved your life. If it had been up to me, and our vampire laws weren't so strict, I might've let you die for all the laws you broke."

Dr. Case glanced at Dr. Vieira. "Why didn't you let me die?"

Dr. Vieira wiped his glasses on his lab coat. "Leroy, we don't kill humans or leave them to die."

Dr. Case dropped his gaze to his lap. A second ticked by before he looked at me. "I'm sorry, Jo. I was so caught up in my sister's death that I didn't even consider your life."

I couldn't recall if Dr. Case had ever apologized to me for what he'd done. Nevertheless, we all made mistakes. "Thank you. But what would really show me your remorse is to help us do everything we can to stop Edmund."

"If you want to leave, there's the door." Webb's tone softened. "I'll let the guards at the gate know that you're welcome to walk out as a free man. I won't hold you on any charges for what you've done. And let's not forget you are just as responsible for all those humans who Edmund killed while you were helping Patrick concoct a vampire serum."

Dr. Case scratched his brown head of hair. "So I can walk out and not look back?"

Webb gave him a nod.

"Will you tell me who killed my sister as you escort me off base?"

"Not a chance," Webb said, sure and strong. "What's your decision?"

"When will you tell me?" Dr. Case asked.

Webb pressed his strong hands into the top of the lab bench. "When you're ready. But if you walk out of here, then you'll never get your answer."

The lab went eerily silent as Dr. Case's heart raced up the chart. I wanted to slide my hand over to him and read his mind so I could understand why he was trying to fight Webb every step of the way.

We had saved his life. He wasn't in any danger from Edmund while he lived on base. Granted, revenge was a powerful emotion. Regardless, I'd gotten to know him more over the last several months, and I didn't want to see anything bad happen to him.

"Leroy," Dr. Vieira said. "You have nothing to go back to unless you want to work for Edmund again. And I don't think you want to help kill innocent humans. You're a good doctor. Put your talent into helping people, not killing them."

Dr. Case let out a loud sigh.

"If you do decide to leave, we can't protect you or help you anymore," Webb said.

Dr. Case hopped off the stool, went over to the sink, and poured himself a glass of water.

"Dr. Case," I said. "We need you. Please stay. You can help us stop Edmund once and for all."

He eyed me over his glass of water. "I do owe you for what I did to you, Jo." Then he pointed at Webb. "We're not finished. I'll stay, but you will tell me what I want to know."

Webb growled, but I caught his hand. Image after image of me in that coffin flickered through his head. Suddenly, it became clear to me that Webb wanted Dr. Case to pay for trying to kill me.

Webb snagged his hand back. "Dr. Vieira, a minute."

I sighed, thankful that the tension in the room had snapped.

Dr. Vieira unbuttoned his lab coat. "Sure. I need a break. Let's walk down to the mess hall. Leroy, keep trying different strains. I'll be back in thirty minutes, then you can take a break."

The three of us walked out.

"Why won't you tell him who killed his sister?" I asked Webb.

"He doesn't need to know right now."

I wanted to know. But who killed Ella Case wasn't important to our mission, and we had a lot to discuss before we took down Edmund.

5

WEBB

The mess hall was quiet with only the chefs preparing the food for the lunch crowd that would start arriving about an hour from now. I sat down at a table near the window, while Jo snagged a chef's attention and ordered a food item. Dr. Vieira poured himself coffee at the drink bar.

I stared out at the courtyard, watching the wind blow the leaves around, much like the conversation with Dr. Case swirling in my head. He could've walked out if he'd wanted, and I would have let him only to have him tailed. He'd heard and seen too much for me to risk any more lives, especially if he teamed up with Edmund again. Then our missions would be compromised.

Dr. Vieira returned with a steaming mug of coffee. "You need to ease up on Leroy. He's been a big help to me while you were away. And I would like to keep him around for a while longer."

"I'm only letting him stay because he knows too much. We can't afford for him to fall into the hands of Edmund."

Dr. Vieira sipped his coffee. "Do you really know who killed Ella?"

I checked on Jo. She was now showing the tall skinny vamp with the chef's hat her ring. "Enough about Ella."

"Webb, think about how you would feel if you didn't know who killed someone you loved. Jo, for example."

"Are you trying to piss me off?" I asked as low as I could. I respected Dr. Vieira, but my patience had been running thin ever since Steven was taken into custody. Maybe filling in for him was a blessing in disguise. I'd always wanted to climb the military ladder, but I was quickly finding out that politics and all the other bullshit that came along with commanding not only my team, but all other military personnel, was exhausting. I definitely had more respect for Steven now.

Dr. Vieira leaned in. "I'm trying to knock some sense into you. We all know that Dr. Case did things he probably regrets and that are against the law, but he's helping us."

I trusted no one. "How do you know he isn't the mole we've been looking for?"

"I don't," Dr. Vieira said. "But I've had my eye on him, and he's been a hard worker."

I cracked my knuckles. "Then make sure he stays a hard worker and nothing else."

Dr. Vieira sat back, slumping his shoulders. "What is it that you wanted to consult with me about?"

"I'm sorry for biting off your head," I said. "We're all under a lot of stress."

"You're a fine leader, Webb. Sometimes I think you're better at the job than Steven. He's more of a hothead than you. But do your job and let me do mine. I promise if I get wind of Leroy doing anything suspicious, I'll let you know."

Nodding, I sighed. "Onto the reason I wanted to chat. Jo's blood packs some serious punch. I'm slowly finding that the more I drink from her, the stronger I get and the more I can read her mind. At first, the effects only lasted when my fangs were in her, but not anymore. What's going on? I've taken blood from her father before in emergency situations, and I've never felt drunk or had any added powers, and we all know Steven has mind-reading capabilities."

Dr. Vieira took a swig of coffee. "We've known that Jo and Sam aren't the average vampires. Frankly, I'm not surprised. Their DNA is unique, and the twins will be able to do things that their father and anyone in their lineage could never do. But it is fascinating that you're acquiring some of her powers."

Jo bounced up, light and happy. "Are you talking about me?"

Man, I would love to see that blinding smile on her all the time.

"In fact, we are," I said. "Remember earlier when you asked if I could read your mind? Well, it seems I can."

She slid into the seat next to me. "For real? Do you know what I'm thinking now?" She covered her hand over mine.

None of her thoughts seeped into me. All I got were her beautiful eyes, ball-squeezing smile, and a mouth I wanted to kiss. "I can't now."

She sighed as though she was relieved.

"Mm," Dr. Vieira said. "So you could earlier but not now. Again, I'm not surprised. Just keep me posted if the effects last longer next time."

Jo twirled her engagement ring, staring off into space.

I leaned in. "What's going on?"

She stopped playing with her diamond. "I've been struggling with how Edmund is able to read minds. You just answered that question. He's got to be drinking…" She shook her head. "Nah. He doesn't have an ounce of my blood. So that couldn't be why."

"He did have your dad's blood," I said. "But if I didn't get any added powers from drinking your father's blood, then Edmund couldn't, either. Right, Doc? Or maybe Edmund has tried Sam's blood. Patrick does have a supply of his."

"But Sam can't read minds," Jo said.

Dr. Vieira placed two fingers on his mouth. "But you two do have the same DNA makeup. Maybe Sam's mind-reading skills haven't matured yet. I've told you that women vampires mature faster than their male counterparts. I wouldn't worry too much about this."

"I disagree," Jo said. "If Edmund can read minds and he does capture one of us, or if we decide that I should take him up on his offer for me to work for him, then he'll know all our plans. We should be making a large supply of Ms. Costner's magical mind-blocking potion instead of the antidote."

"We need both," I said. "I'll contact Alia and ask her to whip up a batch. Doc, keep plugging away on the antidote."

With his coffee cup in hand, Dr. Vieira pushed to his feet.

"Wait. Where's Matthew?" Jo asked. "I thought he would still be here."

"I drove him home last night," Dr. Vieira said. "He's doing fine. No need to worry about him. Oh, and Webb, when I returned from taking Matthew home, Mr. Jackson was at the front gate. He wants to get a message to Ben. Apparently, Ben's grandmother passed away recently. Mr. Jackson would like his son to attend the funeral."

Jo sighed heavily. "Ben was close to his grandmother."

I pulled out my phone. "Thanks, Dr. Vieira. I'll handle Ben." First, I had to meet with the team. I texted Tripp to gather the troops and meet me in the war room.

"If you want, I'll find Ben," Jo said.

"Actually, let's meet with Tripp, then we can address Ben's issue."

Within two minutes, Jo and I were walking into the war room. Well, she bounced, happy, smiling, and glowing. I ambled in behind her, hoping she could stay in that state of mind forever. I would do everything in my power to make sure our future was filled with happiness.

Tripp was sitting on the edge of the oblong table at the bottom of the theater-style room, talking to Sam, Kraft, Olivia, and Kodiak, who were seated in the front row.

"Lieutenant," Tripp said, popping to attention.

The others did as well. I wasn't used to them standing at attention every time I walked into a room. But the act came with the role.

"At ease," I said.

Jo glided over to Sam and gave him a hug before she showed him her ring.

Sam's green gaze flitted to me then back to the ring. "Wow, London. You've got expensive taste."

I would give the world to Jo, no matter the cost.

"So you made your engagement official, finally," Tripp said with a laugh in his voice.

He'd been on me to get the ring. Then again, I'd only proposed to her a month ago. Still, he'd been right. And if I were following all the gentleman protocols like my father had taught me, I would have gotten down on one knee that night on my deck when I had proposed.

I grinned at him.

Olivia, Kraft, and Kodiak came over to shake my hand and hug Jo.

"Okay, let's get started." I didn't want to overshadow the engagement. Hopefully, we would have ample time to celebrate. Right now, time was of the essence. Hollings would need our plan on how to take down Edmund.

After everyone was settled in the front row, I sat on the edge of the table, with the heel of my hands pressed into the wooden tabletop, figuring out where to start.

Tripp leaned forward on his elbows, his sandy-blond hair falling out of the leather strap that secured his ponytail. "Let's start with how your meeting went with Hollings."

My best friend knew me well. "Hollings wants us to send someone inside Edmund's operation to gather evidence so we can bring Edmund in. The council is getting nervous. The human government is asking more and more questions, especially with dead bodies surfacing all over the state."

"You mean the CIA," Tripp said.

I reared back. "Did the commander tell you?" The commander had said that Tripp had been talking with Jonah but nothing else.

"No. An Agent Thomas showed up on base this morning. He was probing about the bodies found at the building on the Indian reservation."

My brain ran amok upon hearing his statement as I wondered if Agent Thomas was one of the men working for Edmund. For now, I pushed forward. I would revisit Agent Thomas later. "The larger issue is…" I swept my gaze over my team.

Tripp, Sam, Jo, Olivia, Kraft, and Kodiak waited for my words as though they held a ton of weight. And they did.

Sam tapped a booted foot on the carpeted floor. "Just say it."

Jo's voice entered my head. *We're stronger together. That includes the people in here.*

I blew out a breath. The moment I spilled the news was the moment shit got real. "Edmund has been working with the CIA." I pinched my eyebrows at Tripp. "Maybe Agent Thomas is part of Edmund's team. Anyway, Edmund has negotiated a deal to build vampires or, as the CIA is calling it, super soldiers to fight alongside the human military."

"That's how he's going to rise to power and lead the military," Jo said, the light bulb glowing in her head.

"What the fuck?" Kraft blurted out, his burgundy eyes going wide.

"They can't get ahold of Patrick Mason's research," Olivia said, her tone rising. "They'll have a field day with that."

"So not only kill Edmund, but Patrick has to die too," Kodiak said as a matter of fact.

All of them mumbled about something.

"That's what my dad told you when you two were speaking telepathically?" Jo asked.

I nodded at her. "Chill, everyone," I said loudly. "We've got a lot to cover."

The room fell silent, although their expressions didn't feel silent. I could see their brains working.

"The elders want Edmund alive," I announced.

"Fuck that." Kraft folded tattooed arms over his chest. "The CIA finds out about us, then they're bound to find out about wolves and magic and other parts of our world that they cannot ever know. We'll all become lab rats."

I definitely wasn't about to disagree.

"Easy," Tripp said. "Let's hear the rest of what the lieutenant has to say."

"Tripp," I said. "The commander mentioned that you had been talking with Jonah and trying to get him on our side. Tell me more."

Tripp sat up straighter. "While you were Bruno's prisoner, the commander thought Jonah might have some intel on your whereabouts. The commander believed that Bruno had some connection to Edmund. We tried all kinds of tactics in torturing Jonah, but he didn't budge. So we moved him to vampire headquarters. It was a bust. The vampire is loyal to Edmund."

"It seems the commander may have gotten through to him. Apparently, Jonah overheard a conversation between the commander and Hollings. Edmund killed a human girl who Jonah was in love with."

"Pfft," Kodiak spewed, his moss-green eyes flashing vampire black. "Jonah doesn't have a loving bone in his body. You're not considering using him, are you?"

I lifted a shoulder. "I haven't decided on anything. I want everyone's input before we put together a plan. Hell, we don't even know where Edmund is. He disappeared from the funeral home, and none of our spies on the streets have seen him."

"What about Nicki?" Olivia asked.

The mere mention of her name made me wince. Nicki had been a thorn in my side ever since the one time I'd dated her.

Jo muttered something under her breath with a smile on her face.

"For all we know, Nicki is with Edmund," I said.

Jo cleared her throat. "Then call her and find out."

My eyebrows went up. Jo was extremely calm with Nicki's name bouncing around. "Not right now. We have some housekeeping things to do, and I want to formulate a solid plan before we go off in ten different directions. We can't afford to fuck up this mission. We've let Edmund slip through our fingers too many times." While I was in charge, in no way were we going to let Edmund get away. I would kill him before that happened.

"I don't trust Jonah," Sam said. "But with my empath abilities, maybe I can be present while you talk to him. I'll tell you if we can trust him."

I rubbed my growing stubble. "Let's table Jonah for now. We may have another person who we can trust more than Jonah." I eyed Sam. "Remember your buddy Howell."

Sam narrowed his green eyes. "No way. He's a putz."

I held up my hand. "He'll cooperate. Olivia and I did save his life."

Sam bounced his knee up and down. "I want to test him out."

"What about sending me in?" Jo asked.

Tripp angled his head at her. "There's no benefit in you going in. Edmund would know you would only want information."

"Maybe not. Maybe he set up my dad to get him out of the way so I would have the freedom to do as I please," she said.

Sam unfolded his six-foot bulk and shook his head of thick black hair. "Whether Edmund set Dad up or not, you're insane, Sis. Patrick will take all your blood and bone marrow and anything else he needs for his sick plan." He shoved his hands into his cargo pants. "Webb, we don't need anyone in there undercover. We already know what Edmund is up to. We just need to find him and kill him and anyone working for him."

Kodiak was on his feet. "Sam's right. Our plan is to destroy. Nothing else. If we dance with the devil, then we're only setting ourselves up to fail. We're fucking SEALs. We're trained to go in stealth mode, completely off the grid. Lieutenant, you stay behind. The SEALs in this room will handle Edmund. That way, the elders won't give you grief."

I wasn't letting my team take the fall for anything.

Olivia picked at a nail. "I agree too, especially on Patrick. He can't live. The CIA will do whatever it takes to get in his head and also get their hands on his research. Although right now, how much does the CIA know, and who within the CIA knows? How many humans are we dealing with?"

"Why aren't you speaking up or protesting to any of this?" Sam asked Jo.

She shrugged. "We're a team. I'm in with whatever we decide. Although in one breath, I do want Edmund dead. But we need to clear Dad first and get evidence before we kill anyone. That's really the only reason I want to get inside Edmund's operation. Because right now, the dagger that was delivered to the elders has Dad going to prison for the rest of his vampire life."

Sam dropped his head.

I pushed off the table. "All right. Let's sleep on all this. I'll be meeting with Hollings again in a couple of days, and he'll want to hear my plan. With the exception of Tripp, you're all dismissed."

"I'll find Ben," Jo said. "Come on, Sam."

The brother-sister duo left, and I was a little sad that Jo hadn't kissed me. Then again, it was probably best to keep things as professional as we could.

"Later," Kraft said. "I have a wolf to meet."

I glanced at Olivia then Kodiak. They raised their eyebrows and shrugged. Yeah, I didn't want to know. Kraft and his werewolf girlfriend, Crysta, who was also Tripp's cousin, had issues that were none of my business.

Kodiak didn't say a word as he marched out.

Olivia hesitated. "Webb, what about Abbey? Edmund wants his daughter."

I twisted my neck from one side to the other. "I don't know. The commander is the only person who knows where she and her mom are, and unless Edmund breaks into vampire headquarters and reads his mind, he'll never find out."

"I hope so for Abbey's sake." Then Olivia left through a side door.

I worried about the little girl as well. I'd taken a liking to her while she lived on base with her mom. But at the moment, I had other things to take care of, and the commander had assured me Abbey and Rachel were safe. Therefore, I had to trust him.

When Tripp and I were finally alone, I pulled on my hair as I paced.

"Webb, chill. None of what we're going through is any worse than everything we've experienced or fought before now."

We couldn't lose another SEAL. We'd already lost Sloan, Quade, and Crowe. And even though my sister had sided with the enemy, she'd been blood. More importantly, I had Jo to worry about. If I lost her, then my life had no meaning.

Tripp sat back in the theater chair and crossed one leg over the other so that his ankle was resting on his knee. "We didn't discuss the Secretary of the Navy's son."

I took a seat next to him. "Fill me in."

"That agent who was here this morning was also asking if we had any information on the whereabouts of Cory Andrews."

I threw my face in my hands. "So someone directed this agent to us, and I would bet Edmund."

"I told him I had no idea what he was talking about. He argued with me. So I told him to get a search warrant if he wanted access to the base."

I growled. "The authorities have no jurisdiction over the military base."

"They could if they had someone high up in the government who gave them access."

"Where's Cory's body now?" I asked.

"On ice in the weapons room in the basement. We can't release him. He doesn't look human. And as far as why no one has reported him missing, that's a mystery. I couldn't find any news articles or reports that said he had gone missing. I would guess the government is covering his disappearance up. Probably the same people that are working for Edmund."

"I get why Hollings seems scared, although according to the commander, Hollings doesn't know about the CIA or super soldiers. The commander doesn't want us to say a word to them in the event one of them is the mole. And I agree."

"Do you think Hollings is siding with Edmund?" Tripp asked.

"I didn't get that sense, but I'm not one hundred percent sure." I really wasn't. "Look, I'm tired. I need some sleep, and I need to think hard on our plan. But I wanted to ask you before hell broke loose around here. Will you be my best man?"

He slapped me on the back. "I was waiting for that question. I would be honored, man."

"One more thing. If anything happens to me before the wedding, I want you to promise you'll take care of Jo."

Tripp's eyes flashed from bronze to deep black. "What are you saying? You're not dying, man."

I swallowed a large boulder. "I don't plan on it, but I don't have nine lives, either. Just promise me."

His nostrils flared. "You have my word."

I let out a sigh.

Tripp secured his hair back into his leather strap. "Come on, Webb. Let's get a drink. You could use one."

I laughed, and it felt good. "You're right. A smooth whiskey will definitely take the edge off."

I needed something to calm me down. Short of having my way with Jo, which wasn't going to happen, a couple of shots of hard liquor might do the trick, even if for just one afternoon.

6

JO

Sam, Olivia, Tripp, and I sat in the viewing room in the first row of the local funeral home. A gentle instrumental melody played from the speakers overhead as fabric rustled from guests shifting in their seats while some quietly wept.

I kept checking the entrance, waiting for my best friend, Darcy, to show. I hadn't seen her since Sam and I boarded Bruno's plane to Alaska over a month ago.

Sam leaned in. "Darcy will be here. She wouldn't miss paying her respects to Ben's grandmother."

"Maybe you should check on Ben and Mr. Jackson."

As soon as we'd arrived, Ben disappeared into another room with his father. He'd been a basket case for the last two days. At first, we hesitated to let Ben out of our sight. But he assured us he was in control of his emotions. As a half human and half vampire, Ben didn't have all the physical qualities vampires had. His problem though was his emotions, which caused his human-colored eyes to turn red whenever his emotions changed. He didn't have fangs, although he had complained about his gums hurting and the hunger for blood. Dr. Vieira had said that Ben wouldn't grow fangs. Apparently, Ben's DNA had shown minimal vampire properties.

Sam buttoned his suit jacket. "I'll be back."

Tripp caught Sam's arm. "Any trouble…" Tripp tapped his earpiece.

Aside from our appropriate attire for a funeral, the four of us were wearing earpieces and armed with daggers, which were securely tucked away underneath our clothing.

"I got it," Sam said as he sauntered out.

I didn't think we would have any trouble. Sure, Mr. Jackson had been suspicious of my dad and wondered why Ben had always shown up in our base infirmary. He'd even gone as far as trying to engage his friend, the chief of police, to investigate my dad. But my dad had contacts in high places within the human government. Regardless, Mr. Jackson was a good man, father, principal of the human high school, and he cared for Sam and me. He'd taken us in when Sam and I had problems with one of our foster parents.

Darcy's cotton candy scent peppered the air. One of the neat things about being a vampire was my ability to distinguish one person from another or a human from vampire.

She breezed over, dressed in black leggings, black boots, and a gray sweater underneath her wool coat. "Mr. Jackson looks awful," she said in a low voice as she sat down in Sam's seat on my right.

"Well, his mother just died," I whispered.

She pulled her long blond hair forward so the strands draped over her chest. "I know that. But maybe I've been around vampires too long."

"Shh," Olivia and Tripp said on my left.

"What do you mean?" I asked.

She huddled closer to me, her human scent tickling my nose and igniting my vampire thirst. My eyes flashed vampire. I always knew when they did because I had a split second of darkness when it happened.

Darcy leaned away from me. "You're not going to bite me, are you?"

"No. Continue." I glanced at the large urn on the table in front of us. Ben's grandmother had been cremated. I wasn't hungry. I just had to calm my system. One human in the room was okay, but a room with more than one human could be a challenge, and there were several sitting behind me. I didn't have an easy way to rid the smell, but focusing on something other than blood helped.

"Anyway, Mr. Jackson has this faraway look in his eyes. It's almost like he's a zombie and barely knows who I am."

Odd that he wouldn't remember her. "He's probably under a lot of stress," I said. "He's been searching for Ben for months. Now his mom is dead."

She sat back against the chair. "You're right. Ben told me his dad found his mom dead at her home. That had to be awful."

Death wasn't pretty, no matter how the person died. I chewed on my cheek as I thought of Kate and how I was the one to kill her. Webb didn't want me to lose sleep over her death, but I did. I didn't know what I would do if he killed Sam, or my dad for that matter. Sure, Kate's death was in self-defense, but that didn't make it any easier for me to deal with. Even when I had killed Blake Turner in self-defense, I'd felt terrible, although his death was a little easier to handle. He hadn't been my fiancé's sister.

Olivia touched my knee. "Stop fidgeting. You're making me nervous."

I hadn't realized I'd been bouncing my leg. I checked my phone that was sitting on my lap. We had a couple more minutes until the eulogy. I texted Webb. *I miss you.*

Immediately, he responded. *I miss you too. Sorry I couldn't be there. Hollings is due to arrive any minute.*

Good luck, I typed out. Then I added several heart emojis before I clicked off the screen.

Two days had passed since Webb and I met with his team. In that time, he hadn't decided on a strategic plan to raid Edmund's operation. He was still gathering intel. An agent with the CIA was constantly calling, trying to get an audience with Webb. At the same time, Webb's team labored around the clock to find out who within the CIA was working with Edmund and also to locate where Edmund and my uncle Patrick had moved their operation. We suspected Alaska since that was the last Sam and I had heard when we were locked up in the funeral home outside the Indian reservation.

"Oh my God," Darcy said rather loudly.

Tripp, Olivia, and I went into soldier mode, scanning the medium-sized room that had filled up with twenty-or-so guests.

Darcy snatched my left hand off my lap. "When did you get the ring?"

Olivia and Tripp sighed.

"It's gorgeous," she cooed. "I'm going to be your maid of honor, right?"

"Duh," I said. "Didn't your dad tell you?" I should've called Darcy to tell her myself, but I'd been busy with everything going on.

Sam joined us, while the priest, Ben, and Mr. Jackson stepped up to the podium. Darcy was right. Mr. Jackson had a weird look in his eyes as though he was on drugs of some type. His chestnut gaze flickered at me. I waved. He frowned. Then he scanned the room as though he was looking for someone. I followed his line of sight, but no one stood out.

All was quiet. Some guests wiped their noses. Some sniffled. Others had no expressions on their faces as they waited for the priest to begin.

I knitted my eyebrows at Ben, who was dressed in a black suit like his dad. He lifted his broad shoulders at me as though he knew that I was trying to ask what was wrong. Sam had to know. He was an empath so he could read emotions. Then again, we were at a funeral, and the mood was supposed to be somber.

The priest pushed his dark glasses up on his nose. "Thank you for coming. I'll say a few short words then hand over the podium to Mr. Jackson then his son, Ben."

He barely got out Ben's name, when the doors to the room slammed shut. Tripp was on his feet before I could jump up. Then the guests were screaming, "Smoke!"

I sniffed. Definitely smoke.

Darcy grabbed onto me. "What's happening?"

The only way out was through the doors that Tripp and Olivia were trying to open.

"We're dead," Darcy cried. "There are no windows or another way out."

The room filled with smoke quickly, and my sharp vision as a vampire was useless. People coughed, cried, and screamed. I was beginning to believe that Darcy was right. We were dead, but I couldn't think like that. I had to help in some way.

I ran up to Tripp and Olivia as I choked. "Break it down."

"If we do, we're walking into a blazing inferno. Not good for us vampires."

"Nor for humans," I said. "We have to get everyone out of here."

Boom. Boom. Boom. The building shook from its foundation. I waved my hands, trying to cut through the smoke so I could see what was causing the persistent banging. I could barely see Ben and Sam punching their fists through the back wall. I grabbed Olivia and Tripp.

The three of us joined them, and we all punched holes in the Sheetrock. In less than a minute, daylight sprayed in through the large hole that led to the back porch of the funeral home.

"Come on," I said to the people who were waiting to race out.

Once we were all outside in the crisp, cool air, people gasped for breath, including me.

I scanned the crowd but didn't see Mr. Jackson. "Where's your dad?" I asked Ben.

He flew back into the burning building. I started after him, when Tripp grabbed me by the waist.

"Not so fast," Tripp said. "Webb would have my head if I let something happen to you."

I laughed, more out of nerves than anything.

Ben emerged with his father's limp body in his arms. He stalked across the parking lot to a lawn on the other side of the street.

Sam and Darcy guided the priest and the other guests away from the funeral home, not far from where Ben was kneeling over his dad.

Olivia was on her phone. I shrugged out of Tripp's hold and was about to dart across the street to Ben, when I spotted a familiar figure leaning against a stop sign a block down from the funeral home. I ran toward Nicki, fury eating at my gut. As I snatched the dagger from the inside of my jacket, my fangs lowered, sharp and deadly. I was about to end the woman once and for all.

She raked her gray gaze over me. "Why won't you die?" she asked seriously. "Cutting the brakes on the limo didn't work. Then my plan for Ben to kidnap you so he could have you all to himself and I could have Webb didn't work, either. And now you walk out of a fire. What's it going to take for you to die?"

My head spun at finding out that she was the culprit who cut the brakes. I wasn't surprised she was trying to kill me, but I was shocked that she would want Webb dead, especially if she loved him. "You love Webb. Why would you want him dead? Unless Kate asked you to kill him."

She snarled, showing her fangs. "He's better off dead. That way, no one can have him."

"You're sick."

She pushed off the pole. "I'm not sick. I want revenge for everything you've done to ruin my life. You killed my best friend, and you took the one man I ever loved away from me."

I squeezed the handle of the dagger so tightly that I could have sworn the weapon would become part of my hand. "Webb was never your boyfriend. And as far as Kate, I'm sorry. But if someone was trying to kill you, then you would protect yourself."

She lowered her gaze, her black hair falling forward. "Are you going to use that dagger on me?"

Boy, I wanted to, but we were standing on a city street with humans around, although the area was quiet save for the guests who were choking and crying. Regardless, I couldn't tell if anyone was lurking in the windows of the homes and buildings along the street. Besides, I didn't want to bring any more attention to the growing list of shit we had to deal with.

Sirens whined in the distance.

"Nah. One, you're not worth it. And two, I would rather throw you in prison, where you'll suffer for the rest of your life."

She threw her back and laughed.

With vampire speed, I grabbed her arm. Then before I could move, a burning pain ricocheted through my body, making me gasp for air. My vision blurred as I tried to stay upright. Nicki cackled like the Wicked Witch of the West, a sound that grated on me but kept me from passing out. The more she roared with laughter, the easier it was for me to keep my eyes open. I flailed a little, trying to latch on to the stop sign pole. Then she shoved me, still laughing. I stumbled, tripping over my own feet. I managed to stay halfway upright as I found an anchor in the building with a large glass window.

I planted my hands on the window as I locked eyes with a very frightened lady, whose eyes were wider than… I couldn't think.

"How does it feel to get a dagger through your heart?" Nicki asked in a condescending voice.

Someone screamed my name, but his voice was muffled as though he was far, far away. I turned around, sliding down the window until my butt was firmly planted on the cold ground. I shivered as I tried to grip the pommel of the dagger that was protruding out of my chest.

Ah, crap. Not again. The last time I had a dagger in me, my instinct was to remove the blade as fast as I could. But for some reason, my arms were weak. The bright-blue sky was fading to a gray color.

Then Tripp's voice boomed in my ears. "Olivia, get Nicki out of here. Sam, get the car."

I shook my head, blinking several times, trying not to pass out. I fell to one side. Then the world went black.

WEBB

Hollings unbuttoned his suit jacket before he sat down on the couch in the commander's private office that was tucked away in the main building far from the control room. The less ears around us, the better.

He crossed one leg over the other. "What have you decided?"

I grabbed the folder that Tripp had given me off the desk. It contained the details of Cory Andrews. I wasn't about to spill a ton of information to Hollings, but he did need to know about Cory and the CIA agent who'd been poking around.

I extended the folder to Hollings as I sat in a chair opposite him. "The human we brought in with Matthew Costner didn't make it."

He scanned the contents of the folder. "Who knows about this?" His tone was even.

"My team, Dr. Vieira, and Dr. Case. And we do have a CIA agent poking around, asking questions about the fire on the Indian reservation."

He cocked his dark head. "CIA? I knew the local police were questioning the bodies they found, but not the CIA."

"So, you know nothing about the CIA?"

A deep crease lined the area between his brows. "Absolutely not."

I rested my elbows on my knees. "Greg, let's be frank with one another. The CIA throws a whole new wrinkle into our operation. If they got their hands on Patrick's research, think about what would happen to our community of vampires. Do you really want humans to find out that we're building vampires?"

He loosened his tie. "I need a drink."

I flicked my head to the credenza on the other side of the office. I could use some more of the whiskey Tripp and I had sampled the other day. My nerves were still ragged. Even with Jo snuggled up to me the past two nights, I hadn't been able to sleep. My mind was working overtime, trying to formulate my next step. We had too many working parts that were scattered all over the place. We didn't know where Edmund was located. We didn't know anything about the CIA or the agents involved. We didn't even know how to clear the commander of the murder charge. Everything was threatening to crash down around us, and if we weren't focused in our fight to protect the vampire community, humans, and our loved ones, then our existence would be compromised. I couldn't let that happen— no matter the law.

Hollings poured two glasses of whiskey. I walked over to the large window that had a view of the prison building across the courtyard. Hollings joined me, handing me a glass. We both sipped the amber liquid as we watched the prison guard pace back and forth in front of the entrance to the prison.

"Do you have a plan set on how to take out Edmund?" he asked.

I cocked an eyebrow. "Now you want me to kill him?"

He sighed heavily. "I don't want the CIA to get their hands on any research that Edmund has. That would be a disaster. So if it means burying the fucker once and for all, then I don't give a damn about what the other elders say."

At least he was thinking clearly. "Look, Greg, before I dive into anything, I have to find the mole within our organization. I'm not moving forward until I do. We've lost too many men. Hell, losing one soldier is too many." I took a swig of whiskey, the smooth liquid barely burning on the way down. "With your permission, I would like to have Steven read the minds of you and the other elders. That way, we can rule out anyone in the council being the mole."

The elders had a cardinal rule—Steven wasn't allowed to read their minds. Actually, he couldn't be anywhere close enough to even brush up against them.

I waited while Hollings nursed his whiskey, staring out the window. If he flat-out said no, then our meeting was over.

"Have you ruled out everyone on your team?" he asked.

"Not yet, but that's my plan. Jo will start with the SEAL team then work her way through everyone in the control room and anyone else involved in our operation." She didn't know that yet, though.

The door to the office burst open, and Kraft barreled in. "Lieutenant, we have a problem." He darted over to the computer on the desk and typed furiously. "Look." He got out of the way so Hollings and I could see the screen.

A local news station showing cop cars and an ambulance filled the screen. In the background, Ben was on his knees at his father's side. My heart rate shot up the charts. The headline read, "Local stabbing in broad daylight."

My phone rang. "What happened?" I asked Tripp in a shaky tone. "Where's Jo?"

"We're coming through the gate now. Get downstairs." The phone went dead.

I flew out of the office until I was outside. The SUV was screeching to a halt. Olivia jumped out of the passenger side and opened the back door. I gasped as I wobbled on my feet.

Jo's limp body lay across Sam's lap. Her shirt was blood soaked.

No. No. No. This couldn't be happening. Suddenly, I couldn't breathe.

Kraft and Hollings drew up alongside me.

"What in the world?" Hollings asked.

I couldn't speak. I couldn't even move.

Sam passed Jo to Olivia, and my heart stopped.

"She got stabbed in the chest," Olivia said as she started for the entrance. "We pulled the dagger out, but she's got an extremely weak pulse."

I held out my trembling hands. "Give her to me," I ordered.

"Lieutenant, I'll take her up to the infirmary." Olivia tipped her head to the SUV. "You need to deal with her."

When my gaze landed on Nicki, I went into soldier mode. *Kill. Kill. Kill.* I stomped over to her, but Tripp blocked me.

"I'll take her to a jail cell," he said. "Go be with Jo. We can interrogate Nicki later."

I growled deeply and bared my fangs at the woman who had made my life a living hell.

Nicki smirked as though she was itching to fight with me. Oh, she would, but I would be the one tearing her apart.

"Webb." Sam's deep voice resonated. "Listen to Tripp. I'll go with him. Take care of my sister. We'll be up shortly."

I was surprised Sam was so calm. He'd always protected Jo, and he always went out of his mind when someone dared to hurt her. Or maybe I was too crazed to see that he was just as furious as I was. It didn't matter. I would deal with Nicki later. That much was certain. For now, Sam was right. I had to be by Jo's side. I couldn't lose her.

In vampire speed, I was shoving open the doors to the infirmary. "Where is she?"

Dr. Case pointed to the first room on the side wall.

I ran in and sucked in a sharp breath. "She's dead, isn't she?"

Dr. Vieira was checking her vitals. "Calm down." His voice was soft.

Thank God he wasn't flipping out like I was. My insides felt as if someone had taken a sledgehammer and rammed it into my gut a thousand times. It didn't help to see blood soaking Jo's shirt, either.

"Talk to me, Olivia. What went down?" My voice didn't even sound like me. The last time my voice had been so shaky was when I learned my parents had been murdered.

Olivia wiped her sweaty forehead with her hand. "Everything happened so fast. The viewing room at the funeral home filled up with smoke. When Tripp and I tried to open the doors, they were locked. People panicked. Then Ben started punching through a wall. With our help, we managed to break an opening to get everyone out. I was ushering the civilians to safety when Jo took off. The next thing I know, she's on the ground with a dagger in her chest."

I stepped up to Jo's bedside. She looked peaceful with her long lashes fanned out over her silky cheeks. I clutched her cold, clammy hand then raised it to my lips. "Please, please, come back to me." She couldn't die. We still had to get married. I still had so much to show her.

Dr. Vieira pulled out a key from his lab coat. "Olivia, go into the fridge in my office." He tossed her the key. "I need two bags of blood that have Jo's name on them."

Olivia disappeared.

I traced circles on the back of Jo's hand. "Is she going to make it?"

Dr. Vieira's face paled. "Not sure. But she's lost a lot of blood, and her pulse is nil."

The heart monitor he'd hooked up to Jo barely registered a heartbeat.

"How is Jo still alive if she had a cobalt dagger in her heart? This is the second time now."

Dr. Vieira pressed his stethoscope to her chest. After a few seconds, he shook his head. "We don't know that the dagger punctured her heart the first time or this time. I suspect though that the first time, the dagger missed. Otherwise, she wouldn't be here. The fact that she's got a weak pulse indicates to me that the blade punctured the sac surrounding her heart. Much like what happened to you when Kate drove the sword into your heart." He opened Jo's blouse and proceeded to check the cut around her left breast. "The problem is the wound isn't closing. It should at least close a little until she drinks fresh blood, then the wound will seal."

He wasn't making me feel hopeful.

"I need to see what her heart is doing. I'm going to insert a scope into her and take a look around."

As I rubbed Jo's hand, blood pooled in the hollow of her stomach. "You have to save her." My eyes burned with tears.

He glanced at me with sad, dark eyes. "I'm sorry, Webb. There are some injuries a vampire can't recover from, and she's losing too much blood."

Growling, I pivoted on my foot and punched the wall, my fist going deep inside the Sheetrock.

Olivia ran in. "Doc, your refrigerator is empty. Not one ounce of blood in there. Are you sure you had Jo's blood?"

Dr. Vieira bolted out of the room.

Olivia and I exchanged a horrified look. I knew he kept blood in his fridge for all of the SEALs in case of emergencies. I also knew he kept reserves of Steven's, Jo's, and Sam's blood. He'd been studying the twins' DNA since they became vampires.

I hurried out with Olivia on my heels. I found Dr. Vieira frozen with one hand gripping the fridge door as he stared at empty shelves.

"Doc," Olivia said. "Who else has a key to your fridge?"

He slammed the door shut and scurried to his desk, where he slid out the top drawer then stuck his hand inside. "The spare is gone. I kept one taped to the underside of the desk."

"Take my blood," I said. We would figure out who stole his key and the blood later. Jo's life was hanging in the balance right now.

Dr. Vieira stomped by me. "She can't have yours. We're dealing with the heart, so she needs her own blood. That's why I keep reserves on all of you. That's how you healed from your heart wound. Get Sam up here." His voice was coated with fury.

Olivia whipped out her phone before I could.

I trailed behind Doc as he scanned the lab then checked each of the hospital rooms.

"Who are you looking for?" As soon as I asked, my brain kicked into overdrive. "Dr. Case?"

"Find him now!" he shouted.

I dove into action, calling Kraft. "Lock the base down and find Dr. Case." He'd been there a couple of minutes ago. I growled so loud that the glasses on the lab bench shook. I had two people to kill today, and they would die slow deaths if Jo didn't live.

Sam flew through the doors. "What's going on?"

"Get in that room at the end," Dr. Vieira ordered.

Sam did as he was told.

Since I couldn't do much for Jo at the moment, it was time to go hunting. Dr. Case was about to get his head bashed in before I interrogated him. And if I was right and he was the mole, then he wasn't going to live to regret a fucking thing.

"Olivia, check Case's quarters. I'll head down to the control room."

She and I ran out. Within a minute, I was down in the control room, standing over Sawyer, a vampire who had a kaleidoscope of eye colors. Jo always loved talking with Sawyer so she could watch his eyes change colors.

"Bring up the perimeter of the base near the woods," I ordered.

While Sawyer's fingers flew over the keys, I picked up the desk phone and called the front gate. When the line connected, I said, "This is Lieutenant London. Don't let Dr. Case leave the base." I hung up and snagged a radio off of Sawyer's desk. "Kraft, check in."

"Olivia called me. Kodiak and I are sweeping the base," Kraft said.

"Good. Sawyer will call if he spots anything on the cameras."

"Ten-four," Kraft said before the radio went silent.

The phone on Sawyer's desk rang. He lifted the receiver. "Yes. One minute." He handed me the phone. "It's Elder Hollings."

I'd forgotten about him. "What is it?"

"How's Jo?"

I held back all my emotions, especially anger, or else I would kill someone. "Not good. Look, we'll need to pick up our conversation another day."

"I'm not leaving until I know how she's doing. What can I do to help?"

I clutched the back of my neck. "Get her father out of jail and on this base ASAP. She might need his blood."

"I'm on it." He hung up.

The radio crackled, then Kraft's voice blared through. "I got him."

I almost collapsed against Sawyer's desk. Instead, I pushed the button on the radio. "Bring him into the interrogation room."

Tripp stalked in with blood above his left eye. "Nicki is out of control."

I wasn't surprised. "Did you get anything out of her?"

He wiped the blood that was about to drip into his eye. "Not a damn thing."

Nicki would talk even if I had to torture the woman.

Kraft pushed Case through the door. Case stumbled down the stairs of the landing. Fear jumped off the man in waves.

Tripp reared back, pursing his lips with a what-the-fuck expression.

I stalked over to the human. "Apparently, Dr. Case wants to die today." I grabbed his arm and hauled him into the interrogation room behind Sawyer's desk. Once inside, I shoved him hard. He flew over the table before falling to the floor.

Then I stomped out, locking the door behind me.

"Aren't you going to talk to him?" Kraft asked.

Tripp, Sawyer, Kraft, and the others sitting at their desks stared at me. Most had no expressions on their faces. Two female vampires, however, resonated with fear. They were lucky Commander Mason wasn't there. Steven would have no doubt broken everything in sight, and not from throwing things or punching walls like I wanted to do. All he had to do was get so angry that his telekinesis alone would be destructive.

"I'm going to let him stew for a minute." I had to take a breath before I questioned Case. "Sawyer, let the front gate know we got Case. Kraft, you and Kodiak get over to Case's quarters and help Olivia search his place. Tripp, I want you with me. Oh, and Sawyer, see where Hollings is on getting the commander back here." I stalked up to the landing that overlooked the entire control room. "I want everyone's attention."

The sounds of pounding keys stopped. Whispers died, and all eyes were on me. I pinned a look on each man and woman. "There's a war brewing, one that threatens our existence."

Pinched eyebrows, open mouths, and straight postures came from every vampire in the room.

"So to prepare for battle, each of you will be subjected to having your mind read to confirm your commitment to this team. If you have a problem with that, then you're free to leave now." My tone was deep and commanding. "Keep in mind that anyone who does leave cannot return. You'll be discharged immediately." *And under surveillance.*

A hum of protests zipped around the room.

I lifted my hands. "Quiet. There's no room here to complain. I'm giving you the option to walk out of here right now."

One of the two females who had fear written all over her face stood up. Her voice shook as she spoke. "With all due respect, Lieutenant, it's an invasion of privacy."

I stifled a growl as I read her name tag. I knew most of the vampires in the control room by name, but the newer ones like Petty Officer Slay I hadn't committed to memory. "Do you have something to hide, Petty Officer Slay?"

She lowered her gaze as she stood at attention. "No, sir. But my personal life is my own."

Sawyer rose. "Donna, you heard the lieutenant. We're at war. We have to put our personal lives aside. I'm not happy about someone reading my every thought, but if it means saving lives, then so be it. And let's not forget we've lost quite a few of our comrades lately."

Following on Sawyer's heels, vampires rose to declare their agreement with Sawyer.

Petty Officer Slay slumped her shoulders.

I made my way over to her. "Slay, Jo won't be in your head long enough to see all your memories. And rest assured, what she sees will not be disclosed, even to me or the commander."

"Thank you," she said as she rolled her chair over to her computer.

The sounds of voices, beeps, and the tapping of keys resumed as I met Tripp at the door to the interrogation room.

"Nice speech," he said. "And nice plan."

I nodded then called to Sawyer. "Thank you."

"I believe in everyone in here," Sawyer said.

I wished I could, and part of me did, but I had to be certain.

"Let me check on Jo, then we'll talk with Case," I said to Tripp.

He gripped my shoulder. "Webb, go and be with Jo. I can handle Case."

I knew he could, but I wanted a piece of the fucker. I also couldn't sit in Jo's room and wait. It was too painful. I did want to be there the minute she woke, if she did. *She will,* a voice in my head said. I prayed that my subconscious was right, because if Jo didn't make it, then my life was over, as was Nicki's and Case's.

8

WEBB

I called up to the infirmary and found that Jo's status hadn't changed. So before I ripped out Case's heart, I went into the kitchen on the other side of the control room and plucked two bottles of blood out of the fridge. I decided to fuel up. Otherwise, I wouldn't just rip out his human heart. I would drain Case of all his blood, and I couldn't do that until I got answers.

Tripp came in, rubbing a finger over one of his fangs. "Not a bad idea."

I grinned. "Good to know we're both thinking alike. Anything wrong with your fangs?"

He stuck his head into the fridge. "Nicki tried to yank them out of me."

I almost spit out the blood. "What the fuck?"

He twisted off the bottle cap. "I shit you not. You better be ready to tango with that feisty bitch. How did you even date her?"

I rested against the counter. "Dude, it was only once, and I knew then that she was trouble. But I swear if Jo doesn't make it, I'm going on a killing spree. First, Case. Then Nicki."

He knocked back the blood as though he was downing one of

the many glasses of whiskey he and I had drunk the other night. "I won't stop you."

I chugged one bottle then the other, and within a second, my nerves settled somewhat. I tossed both bottles into the trash. "Let's go have some fun."

I found my leather strap in my back pocket and tied my hair into a low ponytail. Tripp followed suit. We both took long strides around the perimeter of the room, passing cubicle after cubicle, until we arrived at the interrogation room. Before I could even think about my next move, I barreled in and hauled Case to his feet.

Tripp ran in and pulled me off him. "I'm all for you killing him, but let's get answers first."

I shrugged out of Tripp's hold and created distance between Case and me. The small windowless room was more than suffocating, especially with a human who could be responsible for Jo dying.

Dr. Case puffed out his cheeks as he backed himself into a corner. Tripp folded his arms and settled against the wall adjacent to the door.

I scrutinized the human doctor, itching to tear each strand of his brown hair out of his head, one by one. As if he knew what I was thinking, he gasped.

I paced near the door. "You're lucky Tripp is in the room with me."

"I'm sorry," Dr. Case said.

I growled, showing my fangs. No apology would help the human. He needed to know that in this room devoid of furniture, vampires were on top of the food chain, and the fear on his face confirmed as much.

"Let's start at the beginning," I said. "How long have you been sharing information with Edmund?"

His eyebrows went up into his hairline. "Who says I was doing that?"

Tripp snarled, the sound deadly.

"So you weren't?" I asked.

Dr. Case's brown eyes shifted back and forth. "You gave me no choice."

I launched myself at him. He squealed as my hands went around his neck. "If you don't start talking, then I will tear out your carotid artery." I pressed my fingers to his neck, my nails ready to slice his skin.

"Tripp," Dr. Case pleaded.

"Doc, answer the lieutenant," Tripp said from behind us.

I let go of the human and removed my dagger from the side pocket of my cargo pants.

"Okay," Dr. Case said, sighing. "Put the dagger away."

"Absolutely not. One wrong answer, and this blade is going into your chest. Now talk."

He slid down the wall then raised his knees to his chest. "Not long after you made me a deal to go through that thumb drive in exchange for who killed Ella, Edmund made me a deal as well. If I fed him information that I learned while working in the lab, he would make me a vampire."

I let out a roar of laughter. He'd expressed another reason humans couldn't find out about vampires. Some humans would want to become immortal.

"Laugh all you want," Case said. "You vampires got it made. You don't get sick. You can barely die. You live the way you want. You kill when you want. You heal quickly. Seriously, put yourself in my shoes." He hung his arms over his knees.

He had all good points. But living among humans for eternity wasn't all sweet and rosy, although it would be if the love of my life didn't die. At that thought, my pulse quickened. "So you want to be a vampire, and you think that Edmund can help you become one?"

He picked at a nail. "No. I know Patrick Mason. He's brilliant. And he will be the one to make it happen. He's the one that's driving this experiment. He's the one that approached Edmund when he got discharged from the military. Patrick is the mastermind. Edmund is just following his orders."

Tripp harrumphed. "Whether Patrick is the leader or not, it still doesn't excuse you from what you've done."

"So I stole blood from Dr. Vieira's fridge," Dr. Case said. "So I gave Edmund some information. So I kept notes of conversations that I overheard. They were light years ahead of me, even with the little tidbits I gave them."

I walked away before I killed him. "You're a fucking moron." I was just as much of a moron for believing that Case would do his job and not make the same mistake twice—pissing me off and trying to kill Jo a second time. "Edmund didn't have Jo's blood or DNA before you gave it to him."

He shrugged. "But he had Sam's. And their DNA is the same. I know. I saw the results."

I folded my arms over my chest. "Wait. Are you telling me you were the one that alerted Edmund when Sam and Jo's physical data and blood samples were sent to the lab in Boston?"

Bruno Almeida had confessed that he had stolen their data from that lab. But we'd suspected someone within our organization had alerted Edmund. It hadn't been a coincidence that the Boston lab was raided the same day I left on our mission to Alaska and the same day Jo was on trial for killing Blake Turner.

"I told Patrick," Dr. Case stated. "Are you forgetting that he and I are friends?"

Tripp rubbed his jaw, his blond eyebrows lifting a fraction. "And are you forgetting that we were the ones who saved your fucking life from your friend, Patrick?"

"Or are you forgetting that you're dying to know who killed Ella?" I locked my jaw so fucking tight that I would have sworn it cracked in several places.

"I know who killed Ella," Dr. Case said with conviction.

"Is that so?" Tripp asked. "Then please share." Tripp's fangs were front and center, and he had the feral look in his eyes that said he was about to become a lethal predator.

Case sat on the dusty tile floor with not an ounce of fear on his face anymore. It was as though the information he had shared was cleansing his soul. Little did he know his soul was about to get staked.

I ran the blade of the dagger along my fingers, waiting for Case to answer Tripp.

Case eyed me. "It was you."

A rumble of laughter escaped me.

"You're so wrong," Tripp spoke up. "Do you want to know, blow by blow, how your sister really died?"

"It doesn't matter," Case said. "I won't believe you. That's why Webb wouldn't tell me when I asked him the other day. You didn't have the balls to even tell me that you were the murderer."

I swallowed hard, breathing heavy, fiddling with the dagger I so desperately wanted to use. Instead, I opened the door. The cool air of the control room washed over my heated face. "Sawyer, get me a laptop and bring up the footage from our last mission in Afghanistan." I turned back to Case. "I'll let you decide who killed Ella."

Within a minute, Sawyer handed me the laptop. "It's ready to go. Just hit enter." Then he left.

Dr. Case hopped to his feet. I held the computer, then hit enter. Case pinched his bottom lip in between two fingers, his gaze riveted to the screen.

That day in Afghanistan was one fucked-up mess. The wind had been brutal, whipping up everything in sight. We'd been crossing a mountain range and had just reached our stopping point for the night when—*boom.*

I flinched from the sound coming out of the speakers. It felt as though I was right back in the thick of things in the Afghan mountains.

On screen, a human soldier's body flew up in the air before a barrage of bullets hit us. Ella dodged the firefight to help the human, and when she did, she stepped into Edmund's line of sight. Steven, who'd been next to Edmund, tried to prevent a disaster, but it was too late. Edmund let loose, shooting Ella—once, twice, three times.

Case pushed the laptop out of my hands. The computer crashed to the floor.

Tripp dealt with the mess while I fixated on Case, who was wiping tears away with the back of his hand.

"You realize what happened in that video?" I asked.

The video was rather grainy, but there was no mistaking Edmund's red eyes as he held the gun. He was the only vampire we knew whose eyes changed from their normal color to red. Steven's eyes changed from green to silver when he morphed into vampire mode, and Jo's turned from silver to violet, which indicated that Jo and Steven had strong supernatural powers. We couldn't quite figure out the reason Edmund had the unique eye color. Dr. Vieira suspected that DNA played a factor, and that was for certain, but we were all waiting to find out if his eye color meant more in terms of supernatural abilities.

Case punched the back wall. "Yeah, you didn't kill Ella." He shoved his hands through his hair. "I'm such a fucking idiot."

Edmund had said he didn't shoot Ella intentionally, but the video was clear. He hadn't warned her or screamed at her to get down or out of the way. He'd just let loose with his gun. Shortly after that incident, Edmund had started to act out more and more, disobeying orders from Steven, yelling at people because they looked at him the wrong way, and even draining two human soldiers of their blood. It was as though something in his brain had snapped that night.

Tripp stalked out with the remnants of the broken computer.

My ire had waned a smidgeon. "What is Edmund expecting from you next?"

Case banged the back of his head on the wall. "Edmund is the least of your worries. Agent Thomas with the CIA is who you should be worrying about."

At that moment, Tripp came back in. "Webb, Dr. Vieira wants you upstairs."

My heart flipped out. "Is Jo awake?"

"He didn't say," Tripp said.

I wanted to rush out, but I had to hear what Dr. Case meant by his last statement. "Explain Agent Thomas, and make it fast."

"I was told by Patrick to give the blood I'd stolen to him," Case said.

Tripp and I snarled in unison.

Tripp spoke in a low voice as he stepped closer to Case. "Are you telling us that the CIA—the humans—have our vampire blood?"

The blood Dr. Case had stolen wasn't just Jo's or Steven's or Sam's. The blood reserves included all the SEALs, complete with our names, dates of birth, and special powers. All that paled in comparison to what the human government would do with our blood.

I dove at him. "Do you know what you've done?"

Tripp caught me just in time. "Go, Webb. Now. Jo needs you. I'll handle the rest of this interrogation."

At the mention of Jo's name, I let out a heavy breath. Nevertheless, I punched Dr. Case right in the jaw. He landed on his ass.

"Feel better?" Tripp asked.

I marched out. "Not in the least."

Fuck. The humans had our blood. We were so screwed if the agent didn't give that blood to Patrick. I wondered if Edmund knew what Patrick had done, although Case had just said Patrick was in charge. I found that hard to believe given Edmund's staunch mission to lead an army.

Steven was going to make the earth move, literally. With his elemental magic, he could move earth, air, wind, and fire. Heads would roll, not only at the hands of Steven, but me as well.

As I rushed out, I sucked in lots of air, trying to keep my pulse from soaring off the charts. *Focus on Jo.* That was my problem. I was deathly afraid to walk into her room, afraid to hear Dr. Vieira say she didn't make it. If she was doing fine, then he would've said so when he called down to the control room.

I jogged through the deserted halls and into the lab until I was standing in the doorway to Jo's room. Dr. Vieira was staring at the computer screen that sat on a cart with wheels in front of Jo's bed. My vampire beauty was extremely pale.

"Please tell me good news. Did the cut close?" I didn't cross the threshold. My heart was beating so hard against my ribs, and my body was on the verge of collapsing.

"I'm sorry. I can't give you good news." He didn't take his eyes off the computer screen. "Sam's blood did help a little, but the laceration is still leaking blood. But I do want you to see this." He lifted his head as he pointed to the screen.

I inched over to him like a snail, not sure what to expect.

"I inserted a scope into her." Excitement laced his tone.

Beyond the screen, her white sheet had large spots of blood around her heart. I dragged my gaze to the screen, holding my breath. "What am I looking for?"

He took out his penlight. Then he drew an imaginary circle close to the screen and around Jo's heart. "As vampires, when we get staked with a cobalt dagger, the cobalt starts to burn the muscle, and eventually, the heart shrivels up and stops beating. There are no signs of the muscle being charred or burned, which tells me the blade didn't pierce her heart. And if you look at this area here"—he pointed to a spot below the heart—"there's a small lesion. The blade went through the sac."

I pinched my eyebrows. "Then why isn't it beating?"

"It is." His voice rose in pitch. "Her pulse is at a half a beat per minute. And it's weak because that wound isn't healing. Neil's blood would help in this case, but even his reserves are gone."

Neil Foster had been a comrade until he'd met his death on a mission months ago. He'd been a great soldier, but more importantly, he was the only vampire we knew whose blood had healing properties.

"At that heart rate, she'll be brain dead," I said. However, I wasn't a doctor, so I really didn't know what I was saying.

"Not as a vampire, but she has slipped into a coma, and that's a good thing. Time might heal the injury as her system tries to recover, and it will give me time to find a solution. I thought Sam's blood would do the trick, but as you can see, it hasn't done much. As a temporary fix, I'm going to stitch the wound. Since I don't have Neil's blood, Steven's blood has some healing properties, but his is not as strong as Neil's. When will Steven be here?"

As vampires, our genetic makeup would eventually dissolve the stitches before our skin knitted back together.

"I'll check." Before I did, I traipsed over to her bedside, leaned over, and kissed her on the lips, wishing I were that prince in Snow White who woke his love with one kiss. "Please don't die on me, angel. I need you so badly. I haven't even begun to show you how great our lives will be together." I kissed along her jaw to her ear. "I love you." As tears slid down my face, I pulled out my phone and dialed Hollings.

"What's Steven's ETA?" My voice was shaky.

"We have a problem," Hollings said. "Steven and Jonah are gone. They're not in their cells. We checked the building, and there are no signs of anyone breaking in or breaking out. It's as though the two of them teleported."

No vampire could teleport. Steven had to have used something seriously compelling for the guards to open the doors, but I didn't care how he'd gotten out.

"I'm not sending out a search team," I said. "My gut is telling me the minute I do is the minute Edmund attacks." That was Edmund's mode of operation. He'd done it once before. He'd made us believe he was at one location only to be on base, where he had blown up buildings and kidnapped Jo.

"I got this handled," Hollings said. "How's Jo?"

"Not good. Keep me posted." I hung up.

"I heard," Dr. Vieira said. "I can keep using Sam's blood. His seems to kick up her heartbeat a little at least. He's lying down, resting from the first round. He should be ready to do another round soon."

Soon was too long. "If Sam's blood is barely working on her, then Steven's might not, either. Give her my blood."

He regarded me. "Webb, I've been testing blood, DNA, and our genetic makeup for many, many years. I know what your blood is capable of as well as the entire military team of vampires on this base. Again, since Neil isn't alive, I need her father's blood. Sam just hasn't matured enough yet as a vampire for us to know if his blood will have healing properties. So unless you know of someone who I don't, I'm sorry."

I clenched my jaw. I didn't want to hear how sorry he was. I wanted him to fix Jo. "She's my life, Damon. I can't lose her."

He came up to me and rested a hand on my shoulder. "Webb, I know." His voice was thin.

"What about Tripp?" I asked. "He has a touch that calms people. Try his blood."

Dr. Vieira fiddled with the heart monitor. "I've been down that road with him. His wolf lineage helps him heal faster, but I've tested his blood, knowing that wolf blood has healing properties. But in large part, he's more vampire than wolf."

As though a gust of wind had knocked me over, Tripp's cousin, Crysta, popped into my head. "Crysta. Tripp's cousin. She's pure wolf. Try her blood."

"I thought she left town," Dr. Vieira said.

"Let me check." I got on my phone and called Tripp.

9

WEBB

I blinked several times to keep my eyes open as I sat at Jo's bedside. Hours had passed. The day turned to night. Tripp had finally gotten in contact with Crysta, but she'd been on a plane and had to find her way back here. Even then, we weren't sure if her blood could help Jo.

I felt as though I was being hit from all sides, and more than anything, I wanted to ditch the military and take a long-ass vacation. After things settled with Jo, I would make it my first priority to get the evidence we needed to clear the commander. Then he could take the helm again and deal with Nicki, who I hadn't attempted to interrogate, Mr. Jackson, who was laid up in a civilian hospital, and the Secretary of the Navy's dead son, who barely looked human, and more importantly, find a way to get the CIA out of our business.

I yawned.

The only comforting news was that Jo's heart was still beating at a half a beat per minute. Sam had given her another round of his blood over an hour ago, but there had been no change in Jo's condition, not even her heart rate. As vampires, our hearts beat between five and twenty beats per minute, depending on when we turned vampire. Considering Jo was less than a year in vampire age, her heart rate should have been somewhere in the range of ten to twenty beats per minute.

Footsteps padded in. I lifted my tired eyes.

"Crysta should be here within the hour," Tripp said. "Why don't you go get a shower? Then catch a quick nap. You look like shit. I'll stay with her."

"Any word on where the commander is?" I asked. "Or did he check in?"

"No. Hollings has a team out searching. We'll find him." Tripp's tone wasn't convincing.

Maybe Steven and Jonah went on the hunt for Edmund. That was the only logical reason in my mind as to why Steven would break out unless someone broke them out and kidnapped them.

Tripp sat down in a chair on the other side of Jo's bed. "Go. I'll call you if anything changes around here."

I pushed to my tired feet. "Thank you." My throat burned. I not only needed a shower, but at least a liter of blood. I'd had hunger pangs for the last two hours but hadn't wanted to move. I kissed Jo on the lips then left.

The lab was quiet save for a machine or two humming. Dr. Vieira was studying a computer screen, and Sam was on his phone, listening to the caller on the other end.

Dr. Vieira glanced up at my approach. "I've been wracking my brain as to why her wound won't close. A doctor I studied under had one case where his vampire patient had the same problem. After he'd gotten injured, his wounds wouldn't heal. In reading the case study, the doctor came to the conclusion that since the patient had been stabbed multiple times in the same area, the injury would take longer to heal."

I tilted my head, holding my breath. She had been stabbed by my sister in the same area not that long ago. "So she'll be fine?"

He kept reading the screen. "Maybe. This was just one case

study. However, the doctor further concluded that some vampires don't heal as quickly because of their DNA." He lifted his tired gaze. "So I suspect that blood with healing properties would speed up Jo's recovery."

We had to find her father.

Sam ventured over with his phone in hand. "That was Ben. His father is awake. He had a mild heart attack. Plus, the smoke inhalation didn't help. But we may have a problem."

We always had problems.

"Mr. Jackson is mumbling about Nicki and fangs, and the ER doctor is questioning what drugs Mr. Jackson might have taken. According to the doctor, Mr. Jackson's dilated pupils indicate drug use."

"Someone compelled him," Dr. Vieira said, returning to his computer screen.

"Nicki," I said through a growl.

What a fucking day!

"Do you want me to head over to the hospital and see what's up?" Sam asked.

I scratched my neck. "No. Call Ben and tell him to bring his father here." The only person who could un-compel Mr. Jackson was the person who'd put him in that state of mind. "After I get Nicki to pull him out, then you can erase whatever she planted in his head."

Sam had the ability to wipe out someone's entire memory or one memory at a time if he knew what that memory was.

Sam walked away, tapping the screen of his phone.

"I'm going to shower. Crysta should be here soon." I stalked out.

The brisk night air swept over me as I trudged through the woods, my booted feet sinking into the dirt and leaves. I tried to clear my mind, listening to the crickets singing and an owl hooting. The dense trees and thicket reminded me of when I'd chased Jo through the woods the night she'd been rescued from her boating accident. Man, that was a night I would never forget. I laughed at the memory of how she'd been hanging upside down from a tree. She'd been caught in one of the traps we'd set all over the wooded part of the base. She'd managed to get free and had been about to jump down when I'd caught her.

A little girl's voice carried on the breeze, jarring me from my memory. I stopped and listened as I sharpened my vision, scanning my house that lay ahead.

"Mander, where's my mommy?"

Abbey? The commander? In a flash, I was walking through my front door.

Abbey ran and jumped into my arms. "I want my mommy." Tears filled her bright-blue eyes.

I held her as she rested her head on my shoulder. So many questions bombarded me, but those could wait.

The light from the side table glowed, highlighting two tired vampires. Steven sat on the couch, and Jonah was on the chair opposite him.

I pinned a glare on Steven.

His eyes shuddered between green and silver. "What's wrong?"

"Jo is in a coma, and—"

He tore out of the house.

With a relieved sigh, I dropped onto the couch with Abbey in my lap. I should've run out with him, but I couldn't leave Jonah in my house or with Abbey. After all, Jonah had been and could still be Edmund's right-hand man.

Abbey snuggled into me as she closed her eyes. Within a minute, she was breathing heavily. Man, I would have given anything to shut my eyes, but if I did, I might not wake up for a month.

The oversized chair Jonah was sitting in seemed too small for his large build. The last time I'd seen Jonah was when we captured him during one of our raids. At that time, he'd been defiant and rabid, which was understandable as an enemy. Yet as he sat with one leg crossed over the other, he gave me the impression that he was a friend and not a foe.

"So, talk," I said. "Tell me why you and Steven aren't in jail and how you got out." Warmth traveled through my body as my eyes grew heavy.

He pointed a large finger at Abbey. "Her mom dropped her off with Steven's attorney with a note that said she was getting revenge and that Edmund needs to die for killing her husband. Once Steven got the message, he compelled every guardian in the building into releasing him. And before we walked out, he erased the footage on the security cameras. I knew he was powerful, but he compelled two and three guards at a time."

Sam could do just that, but I hadn't been aware that Steven could. It didn't matter. "So you busted out. Then what?"

"We got Abbey from Mr. Rose's house. Steven didn't think she was safe, and he wants to stop Rachel."

"How does Rachel know where Edmund is?" We didn't even know that.

"I'm not sure," he said.

I gently untangled Abbey and placed her head on the pillow next to me. Then I pushed to my feet and stalked into the kitchen to grab some much-needed blood. I desperately wanted a shower, but my hygiene could wait. I had to get back to Jo. After I sated my hunger, I collected Abbey.

"Come on," I said to Jonah. "We're going to the infirmary."

10

JO

Rolling green hills spanned out beneath the snowcapped mountains in the distance that climbed high into the sky. Stars twinkled above, bright and large, as I played with the blades of wet grass at my side. I tried to lift my head, but I couldn't move. I felt as though I was glued to the earth. The scent of fire lingered from somewhere. I darted my gaze to the right then left, but I couldn't see anything. I tried again to sit up, and when I did, a large black paw stepped on my chest. I screamed. The agony of pain took my breath away.

A panther came into view, staring down at me with topaz-colored eyes beaming in the darkness. Then another figure appeared —an old man draped in a red robe with a gold sash around his neck. He too seemed to glow in the dark. The panther heeled on my left, and the old man kneeled on my right.

His warm hand grasped mine. "Child, do you remember me?"

I swung my gaze from the panther to the old man, who had black hair, a slender build, and silver eyes that glinted. "I do, but I don't know your name."

He smiled. "I'm your grandfather. I've been watching over you."

I pinched my eyebrows together. "Where am I? Where's my dad? My brother?"

"Shh," he said. "You'll see them soon enough. You need to heal. I want you to rest."

"What happened?" I sifted through my brain but was drawing a blank.

He placed a hand on my heart, and an energy like no other filled me, swirling around as though his hand was inside me, massaging my heart. "You were severely injured." He pressed down on my chest.

I coughed up blood.

"Serapis," he said to the panther.

Before I knew what was happening, the panther was licking the blood from my face. When he was finished, he sat on his haunches, his golden-yellow eyes appraising.

The old man, or I should say my grandfather, helped me to a sitting position. "Better?"

I inhaled deeply, the scent of honeysuckle tickling my nose. "I can breathe again."

"Good. Now listen carefully. You must be more calculating and cautious of your enemy. You must not jump into battle without thinking. I cannot save you again. Listen to your father. Heed his direction, and whatever you do, do not, I repeat, do *not* allow Edmund Rain to live."

"But he won't die, no matter what we do." My voice cracked as my body hummed to life.

"He will, and he will die by your hand. I must go." He floated to a standing position.

"Wait. Why must he die?"

My grandfather swept his hand through the air, the act propelling me to my feet. "He will continue to cause death and destruction for both humans and vampires, and in the process, his daughter, Abbey, will die. If the vampire population is to survive and grow, she is the only natural-born female vampire who will be able to conceive."

"But if Edmund dies, Abbey won't have his blood to turn vampire when she becomes a teenager."

"She's naturally and slowly changing into a vampire as we speak. Her change will be complete when she turns sixteen. No paternal blood is needed for Abbey. Now make sure Edmund dies." My grandfather waved a hand at Serapis. "Time to go."

"No," I said. "I need you by my side."

"You don't need me, child. You need the ones who love you who are alive." He spoke as though I would never see him again.

I felt empty and sad as he and Serapis trekked down the rolling hills toward the mountainside. As their bodies blurred, my chest tightened, my body shook, and I began coughing. A loud beep pounded in my ears among the many voices screaming in the distance. I opened my eyes, squinting at the glaring light that burned my pupils.

"Jo! Jo! Jo!" So many voices were calling me.

"Angel."

"Webb?" Tears shot forward at the sound of his deep, husky voice, a voice I wanted to hear over and over again. But the tears quickly dried as I heaved and coughed until blood dribbled out of my mouth and onto the white sheet.

Someone began wiping my face. "Everyone, get out," Dr. Vieira ordered.

"I am not leaving." Webb's voice was close to my ear.

I blinked to orient my vision, but my stomach heaved again, and again, more blood spilled out.

"Neither am I," my dad chimed in.

Dr. Vieira placed a cup at my mouth. "Drink."

I sipped on ice water. The liquid slid down and cooled my insides, erasing the sandpaper feeling. My vision slowly sharpened.

My head jerked right as my hand reached out to Webb. He leaned in to kiss me on the forehead. My lips quivered, my body shook, and my mind scrambled to make sense of how I got there.

Webb's cobalt-blue eyes, the ones that always sucked me in, glossed over. "I am so fucking glad you didn't die."

I gripped his trembling hand as my eyes adjusted to the bright lights overhead. I slowly gauged my surroundings. A machine beeped from somewhere behind me, and a brief memory flashed of my time in a human hospital thanks to my foster dad, who had stabbed me not once, but twice. Suddenly, the pain from that night melded into the searing, burning pain of the dagger that Nicki had embedded in my chest.

I gasped as anger swished in my stomach, causing my fangs to drop and my eyes to flash vampire.

Dr. Vieira adjusted the IV bag full of blood. "You need to rest."

I needed to kill Nicki. "Where's Nicki?" I threw the sheets off me as I swung my legs over the side of the bed.

Webb blocked me before tucking my legs back under the covers. "As Doc said, you need to rest."

I needed to exact revenge once and for all.

"Revenge will come in time," Dad said from the bottom of my bed.

"Dad?" My mind was a bowl of mush. "Wait. Why aren't you in jail?"

Sam squeezed my toes. "Nicki is sitting in a jail cell in the prison building."

"Nicki cut the brakes on our limo." My voice wavered as pure rage continued to pound against my stomach. Then I thought of Mr. Jackson. "How is Mr. Jackson? Darcy?" Oh my God, my best friend had been almost killed by vampires… again. "Did anyone get hurt at the funeral home?"

"Whoa!" Sam said. "One thing at a time."

Dad traded places with Dr. Vieira, who was fiddling with my chart. His dark-green eyes locked on my diamond. "Beautiful."

Nicki and everything that had happened dulled in the background for the moment as though the diamond surrounded by amethysts had the magical ability to make me smile.

"I have a lot to catch up on," Dad said. "But I'm afraid that I must go."

I angled my head. "Where?"

"Dad broke out of jail to save Abbey," Sam said.

"So you're going back to jail?" I asked. "And what do you mean save Abbey?"

Dr. Vieira pushed Dad to the side. "Enough. Her heartbeat is all over the place, and until she gets some rest, no more talk about enemies, jail, or death."

"We'll talk soon," Dad said.

Webb eyed Dr. Vieira. "Can I have five minutes alone with Jo?"

"Not a minute more." Dr. Vieira started to usher Dad and Sam out of the room.

"Steven," Webb said. "We need to talk before you return to Boston."

"Dad?" I called.

Dr. Vieira glared at me. "Make it quick, Jo."

Sam and Dr. Vieira disappeared, while Dad stood at the foot of my bed. His shoulder-length black hair was mussed around his shoulders, and the lines around his eyes seemed to have multiplied since he was arrested.

"My grandfather told me that I would be the one to kill Edmund."

Dad swayed for a second. "Is he the old man in your dreams?"

I nodded once. "I always knew he looked familiar. Anyway, he said that if Edmund doesn't die, then he'll continue to cause death and destruction, and Abbey will die in the process."

My dad lowered his gaze as though he already knew of the premonition.

"But you know the rest. Don't you, Dad?"

On shaky legs, he sank into the chair in the corner of the room. "I do."

Lines dented Webb's forehead. "What's going on?"

Dad pinched his nose. "Just before my father died, he told me that a little girl would be born who could see into the future before she could even walk or change into a vampire and that she would come into my life when I was least expecting it. But when she did, I was to do everything in my power to protect her."

"Because Edmund would use her for his own lab experiments," Webb said.

"True." Dad sighed. "But more importantly, she is the only natural-born female vampire who will be able to have children that will also bear the natural-born vampire gene."

Up until that moment, I'd never thought too hard about having children or even wondered if I could conceive. I knew vampire children were born to a male vampire and a human female who carried the unique blood type of Vel negative. I also knew that our population was dwindling because of the rarity of human females with that blood type. Nevertheless, I was suddenly sad that Webb and I would never have children. Even so, I asked, "So I can't have kids?"

My dad sighed. "I'm afraid not, pumpkin."

Webb leaned in close to my ear. "We can always adopt."

I wasn't so sure how we could raise a human baby unless our race had children who carried the natural-born vampire gene. Even then, those types of children wouldn't be able to turn vampire, not without the blood of their biological fathers.

"Dad, my grandfather also said that Abbey is naturally and slowly changing into a vampire. She won't need Edmund's blood to make the change, and by the age of sixteen, she will be a vampire."

"Which explains her powers at the age of four," Webb said. "Steven, Abbey shouldn't be near or with Jonah. He can't be trusted. We've had one too many moles among us. My sister and now Dr. Case."

I did a double take. "Dr. Case is a mole?"

"He stole all the reserve blood that Dr. Vieira kept for emergencies," Webb said. "That's why you almost died."

The machines and other items in the room started to shake as my anger rose, or maybe Dad's anger was helping to cause a small earthquake.

"Stop. Both of you." Webb raised his voice. "We need to regroup, figure out how to clean up the problems we have, and prevent other issues from happening. And that means finding and killing Edmund and Patrick. According to Case, Patrick is the one in charge. He's the one that instructed Case to give all our reserve supply of blood to Agent Thomas with the CIA."

The machines and furniture in the room skidded across the floor as Dad flew off the chair. Then he came to an abrupt halt as a whirlwind of fire with long black hair and rosy cheeks swooped in.

"Mander." Abbey jumped into my dad's arms. "There's a real wolf out in the lab."

The tension pinging off the walls vanished as my dad smiled at Abbey. "Is that so? I thought you were my little wolf."

"Nah. I'm a vampire. Why are you sad, Mander?"

"I miss your mom. Do you know where she is?"

She hooked an arm around Dad's neck. "No." Then her blue gaze landed on me. "Jo, I knew you would make it."

"How?" I asked.

When I first met Abbey, she had shown me a vision of me running in the woods from a man with red eyes. I couldn't say her vision had come true, although it felt as if anytime I was running from someone, I was running through the woods.

She puckered her lips and shrugged. "I don't know. I see things. You know, I turned five last week," she said as though I was supposed to know that five was the magic number for her unique abilities to blossom.

I looked at Webb and Dad. "You did. We'll have to celebrate."

She squirmed in my dad's arms. "Ooh. Can I have a pink cake?"

"Any kind you want," Dad said. "Let's go see if the mess hall has some cake. And Jo, I'm glad you're alive."

I was too. I wanted to marry the handsome vampire who looked like death and needed a year of sleep.

When Webb and I were alone, he released a huge sigh. "Finally. I wanted everyone to leave ages ago." He sat on the edge of the bed and leaned in, brushing his lips across mine. "Don't ever do that again. I seriously thought I'd lost you. I've been going nuts."

I flattened my palms on his stubbled jaw. "I'm sorry that I scared you. Kiss me?"

His tongue was in my mouth before I finished my sentence. Tingles coated my body as I returned the kiss. I wanted him to crawl into bed with me, but my eyes were getting heavy.

He broke away, rubbing the back of my hand that wore his engagement ring. "I love you more than you can imagine. Please, please be more aware of your enemies, our enemies. I can't lose you."

The trepidation in his voice caused my tears to surface. "I'm sorry. Everything happened so fast."

"It always does in battle. You need to start wearing an armored vest anytime you leave the base."

The Sentinels had special armored vests, designed to withstand daggers and swords. Regardless, I'd been at a funeral, mourning Ben's grandmother. "How is Mr. Jackson?" The last I remembered, Ben had laid his father down on a lawn across from the funeral home.

"He's fine. Ben is bringing him here to the infirmary. Nicki compelled him. But don't worry about him or anything else right now. I do have some things I need to take care of. Sleep. I'll be back before you wake up."

I grasped his hand. "Wait. How will we capture and kill Edmund and get through every other problem we have? I really would like to get married soon."

Happiness flickered in his eyes at the mention of marriage. "We have the mole. And before we do anything, you and your father will read the minds of every vampire and human on our team. No more moles. This time when we fight Edmund, we will win." The confidence in his tone could have filled ten football stadiums.

We would win, and if my grandfather was right, then I would be the one to kill Edmund.

The hot shower beat down on me, washing all the grime, blood, and grease from my hair and body. I'd slept for a solid twenty-four hours, and when I'd awoken, Webb was right beside me, sitting in the chair next to my hospital bed. I couldn't wait until I woke up to him every morning in our bed at his house in Maine— just him and me, with no enemies on our tails, no moles, no military, and definitely no Edmund lurking in the shadows.

A knock sounded on the bathroom door. "Jo," Dad called. "Hurry up. We're meeting down in the war room in fifteen minutes."

I shampooed my hair. "I'll be there on time."

As soon as I'd woken up that morning, Dad and Webb filled me in on everything that had happened while I'd been on my deathbed. Rachel had left Abbey with Mr. Rose. Dad had broken out of jail to get Abbey because she wasn't safe with humans. Dr. Case was the mole, and he had given all our blood reserves to Agent Thomas. Saying that the shit was hitting the fan would have been an understatement. We needed Dad more than ever, but Hollings was on his way here to escort him back to jail.

I rinsed quickly, toweled off, then darted into my room and combed out my hair. As I was dressing, I checked the spot under my breast, where Nicki had stabbed me. Before I'd left the infirmary earlier, Dr. Vieira had explained to me that my wound wouldn't close and he'd had to stitch it until he could find blood that had healing properties. Thanks to my dad's blood, my skin didn't show any signs that I had been stabbed.

I threw a T-shirt over my jeans, slipped into a pair of Chucks, then headed down to the war room. When I arrived, it was like walking into a swarm of bees. The fury was buzzing around as Hollings, Dad, and Webb stared at Nicki, who was sitting in the first row.

I climbed down the steps in my own world of happiness rather than anger. Sure, I wanted to rip out Nicki's throat, but I had questions for her. I'd rounded the first row, when Webb sauntered up to me. His hair was tied back in a low ponytail, his stark blue eyes were bright, and his grin was sexy.

My stomach fluttered even more when he kissed me.

Nicki snarled.

I was tempted to make the kiss more passionate with my fiancé, but I wasn't there to brag, although the idea of making her jealous did appeal to me.

"You look a million times better," Webb said in my ear. "And smell good too."

I warmed at his words. "What's going on?"

"We were waiting on you." Dad was dressed in his black cargo uniform, ready for battle. "I've been reading minds all night and morning, and I can't do any more. So we need you to get into Nicki's head."

"Are you up for it?" Webb asked at my side.

I was more than ready. Diving into her mind was far better than asking questions that I was certain she wouldn't answer truthfully. I sat down next to Nicki, who was chained to the chair.

She bared her fangs. "Don't touch me." Her dark hair fell over her face as she squirmed, pulling one cuffed arm then the other.

With her vampire strength, she should have been able to break free from the arms of her chair. "Can't she get out of the restraints?"

"She won't break free," Dad said. "Dr. Vieira has given her a mild sedative that will keep her alert, but she will lack the strength to do anything."

I almost wanted her to break free so I had a reason to fight her until the death.

Hollings, dressed in jeans and a black button-up shirt, which was out of place for the elder, cleared his throat. "Let's get this show going. I have questions for her."

"Can we trust you?" I asked Hollings. When Webb and I had met him in his office, I hadn't trusted him.

"I read his mind," Dad said. "He's good. And what we find, he'll keep from the other elders until we can ensure they're not working with Edmund."

I wondered, though, if Hollings knew of Alia Costner's mind-blocking potion.

Dad responded to my thought. "It wasn't blank, Jo. He didn't take Alia's potion."

"Once you read her mind"—Webb went over to the table and grabbed a roll of duct tape—"Sam will erase her memories."

"Hell you will." Nicki spit as she said the words. "You said you wouldn't do that if I removed Mr. Jackson out of his compelling state. I did as you ordered."

What a brilliant idea. Not having any memories would no doubt be horrifying, at least to me.

"Then she's off to a secure prison in Puerto Rico," Hollings added.

Webb ripped off a piece of tape and placed it over Nicki's mouth. "That's so she won't bite."

I drew in a breath then went to work, covering her hand with mine. I closed my eyes and dove into a dark chasm. My eyes flitted back and forth as I looked for an opening or memory. When her hand twitched, I was propelled down the dark hole, the light pulling me forward. Once the darkness vanished and the sunlight beamed down, my muscles tensed at the memory of her and Webb kissing on the deck of his house in Maine. My eyes flew open.

She cackled beneath the tape.

"What is it?" Webb asked.

"Nothing." He didn't need to know what I'd seen. I knew they'd had one or two dates, and that was in the past. I couldn't get jealous, although it was hard not to. I resumed my efforts, shutting my eyes as I tried another tactic. I dug my nails into her warm skin. She groaned, and when she did, the blackness suddenly vanished, and I was on a journey through her mind.

She was jealous that Kate had two men who loved her, Edmund and my dad. She despised me. She loved Webb. She felt bad that she'd had to compel Mr. Jackson into cutting the brakes on the limo. But if she couldn't have Webb, then nobody could. So she had resolved herself to killing him too. She owed Edmund her life. He'd found her and her baby sister foraging through dumpsters behind a bar one night. He'd made her a deal. If she worked for him, he would pay her well. So she had put her sister into a boarding school for girls and started her new life with Edmund. Then images of dead bodies flickered by. One in particular had me gasping.

"Jo," Webb said.

I opened my eyes. "I need a break." Reading minds was tiring and creepy, and I felt every emotion of the person whose mind I was in.

"Did you learn anything?" Hollings asked.

I wiped my forehead with the back of my hand. "She killed that private detective, Diane Wallace."

The air left the room as Dad's rage filled every corner until he was in Nicki's face. "She was a human. She did nothing to you."

Hollings shoved Dad away before he clamped a hand around her throat. "You deserve to die."

Nicki's eyes bugged out as she kicked and squirmed, even more so when Hollings pulled out a dagger from his back pocket and positioned the tip of the blade at her jugular. "Do you want to live?" He ripped the tape off her mouth with his free hand.

She spit in his face. "You'll never get any answers out of me. So kill me."

I found it odd that the elder who wanted us to abide by vampire laws was ready to break one.

Dad clutched Hollings's arm. "Enough."

"She's loyal to Edmund," I said. "She won't tell us anything."

Hollings whipped his dark head around to look at me, his fangs shooting out, almost dripping with venom. "Then read her mind again."

Dad guided Hollings over to the table. "Let Jo handle this."

Webb stood close to me.

"You want to keep your memories," I said to Nicki. "And we want to know where Edmund is."

Hollings wagged a finger at me, his black eyes flooded with rage. "You're not making a deal with her."

A deal was the only way Nicki would listen or help us, especially if she loved her sister.

"Greg," Dad warned, "calm down. We need to clear up all our shit before the humans get their hands on our DNA."

"It's too late for that," Nicki said.

Webb moved to sit on the other side of Nicki. "She's right. Dr. Case has given our blood reserves to Agent Thomas."

Hollings spewed cuss words.

I locked eyes with Nicki "I suspect one of the reasons you don't want to lose your memories is that you'll never be able to find your sister."

Her skin paled. "You saw that part?" Her tone was soft—a stark contrast to her snarky attitude.

I tilted my head. "So if you tell us where Edmund is, then we'll let you keep some of your memories of your sister."

She considered us as she gnawed on her lip. "She knows what to do in the event I die."

I had to applaud Nicki for her staunch dedication to Edmund. If I were in her shoes, Sam would have come first over anyone. Then again, I wasn't sure how I would decide if I had to choose between Webb and Sam, although Nicki wasn't in love with Edmund... or maybe she was.

"Are you in love with Edmund so much that he is more important than your sister?" I asked.

"Absolutely not. But he saved my life. I owe him mine." Her rabid personality had died off. In its place was a more controlled attitude as though she had fought her demons and was ready to die for Edmund.

"Over your sister?" Webb asked in a sympathetic tone. I imagined he was thinking of his own sister.

A tear trickled down her face. "She's better off without me. She's human, anyway. She doesn't need to be exposed to this world, and with our father dead, she'll never be able to make the change."

"Nicki, please," I said. "If you don't want your sister to be part of our world, then Edmund needs to be stopped. If the CIA has our DNA, it's only a matter of time before they start hunting vampires."

We were shifting from Edmund building an army to something far greater and worse than what Edmund could do. The human government's possession of our DNA would be the end of our existence.

"She's right," Dad said. "The CIA agents who are working with Edmund might want to build their own super army. But think about when other parts of the human government find out about us. They won't hunt us down to use us for whatever plan they might have. They'll hunt us down and kill us. And think of the radicals that will be afraid of us. We don't exactly have a great starting point given all the folklore that humans have read about vampires."

One by one, she eyed each of us. "I don't know where Edmund is."

See if she's telling the truth, Dad said telepathically.

I placed my hand on her warm wrist and continued my quest to get answers. I closed my eyes, inhaled deeply, then dove into her mind. I twitched as I quickly passed memories of her childhood. She played with dolls with her sister and watched her father beat her mom. I shivered at how brutal her father had been. Out of nowhere, I was falling into a tunnel. These memories were full of sunlight and images of Nicki seducing Matthew and the human we rescued who was now dead. She even seduced the Secretary of the Navy before she killed him.

My eyes flew open.

Webb was on his knees in front of me, wiping away the sweat sliding down my temples with the pads of his warm fingers. "You've had enough."

I understood why my dad was exhausted from reading minds all night.

Nicki slouched in her seat as though she had just read someone's mind. "So now you know."

"That I do."

Hollings hunched over slightly as though he was ready to pounce. "Well, are you going to tell us?"

I puffed out my cheeks. I should have been blurting out that my father was innocent, which I had highly suspected, but I was trying hard to calm my mind from the wild ride Nicki had taken me on. For some odd reason, seeing her father slap, punch, and kick her mom brought back memories of when I was in foster care. I'd seen one too many men beat their wives, and it always triggered an uneasy feeling, even more so when I became a victim.

I touched my left cheek. The scar was barely visible, but the memory was crystal clear. Suddenly, I was propelled back to that night I'd been alone in my room, waiting for Sam to return home, when my foster dad had snuck in. His stench smelled of booze and cigarettes. His breath reeked of alcohol. His jagged teeth had crud lodged between them. His hands were the size of bear paws as he had touched my legs, inch by inch, until his calloused hands had been replaced by a cold steel blade.

Webb's warm fingers wrapped around my wrist. "Angel."

That horrible and painful night faded until I was staring at the most handsome creature I'd ever laid eyes on.

"You're thinking of that night you got that scar." Webb gently tried to pull my fingers from my cheek, where Cliff had stabbed me.

I slowly lowered my arm. My dad's eyes were in full vampire mode, almost glowing with anger. After I'd told Dad what had happened to me, we'd never spoken about the incident again. Regardless, as I sat next to Nicki, I wanted to reach over and squeeze her hand. I'd only seen one memory of her abusive father. But I would bet she'd been a victim of his abuse.

I gave myself a quick mental pep talk. I was there to get answers, not to delve into my past that had no place in my new world.

I sucked in air, planting on a smile as I touched Webb's rough jaw. "I'm good."

He searched my face as his eyes flickered between blue and black. "No more reading minds today or maybe ever."

I nodded. "No more today." I couldn't say that I wouldn't read another mind again. Sometimes when I touched people, I had no control over probing their thoughts. Some memories just flashed brightly the instant I touched a person.

Hollings clucked his tongue. "Are we ready to get back to the task at hand?"

Dad retracted his fangs, his anger no longer evident. "Jo, what did Nicki show you?"

"I showed her how I killed the Secretary of the Navy." Nicki's words rushed out as though she didn't want me to divulge any memories that weren't pertinent to why she was there.

My father groaned out a sigh.

Hollings lifted his eyebrows. "You?"

Nicki sneered at Hollings. "It's called seduction. A man will do anything with a woman on his lap."

Webb straightened to his full height as he folded his arms over his chest. "Why did Edmund want him dead?"

Her expression softened. "It wasn't Edmund. Agent Thomas with the CIA wanted the secretary out of the picture because he believed in building the military with strong men and women but not something that wasn't human."

"And his son?" Dad asked.

"A guy who overheard too much and wanted to try his hand at becoming a vampire," Nicki said.

"So how did the CIA get involved with Edmund?" Hollings's deep tone reminded me of when he was presiding over my murder trial.

Nicki shifted in her seat. "It was never Edmund. Patrick knows Agent Thomas. Patrick's goal has always been to sell his research to the government, but he didn't have much research when Edmund recruited him. Since then, Patrick has convinced Edmund to bring in the CIA so the human government could fund the labs, equipment, and all the material needed to test. And as far as I'm aware, the agents Thomas and Wyman are the only two who are involved from the CIA."

"And you don't know where Edmund or my uncle Patrick is now?" I asked.

She swung her gaze around the room before settling on Webb, who stood near me. "Before I answer any more questions, I want to make a deal."

Hollings pushed off the table as though he wanted to strangle Nicki.

My dad caught him. "Greg, she's our only resource in getting closer to Edmund. Why don't you take a break? I'll fill you in later."

Hollings growled as he crossed the room and left. Immediately, the air thinned out as though someone had stuck a pin in a balloon.

Dad settled on Nicki's left. "Talk."

"I want my sister taken care of, which means you pay for her boarding school tuition. I also don't want my memories of my sister wiped." She turned to me with pleading gray eyes. "Not even the bad ones with my asshole father. They keep me grounded."

Webb and Dad exchanged a puzzled look.

"Done," Dad said. "Now tell us everything about Edmund's operation."

Nicki slumped her shoulders. "I suspect Edmund is in Alaska. When he ran from the funeral home, I lost track of him. With Kate out of the picture, I suspect Edmund didn't want me anymore. He and I had been arguing a lot lately, and I didn't agree with some of the bonehead tactics he'd used, like the lab on the Indian reservation and keeping Sam and Jo alive."

Webb grumbled at her last statement. Dad didn't flinch, and neither did I.

"You know he kept us alive because he wanted to bargain with my father," I said. It didn't bother me that she'd wanted me dead. The feeling was mutual, although death was easy, and Nicki didn't deserve easy. She should be punished for all the wrong she'd done.

"And that's when Edmund changed. When he learned he had a daughter, he got furious with Kate. He accused her of keeping that big news a secret. He believed she knew. I knew she didn't. If Kate had known about his daughter, then she would've done everything in her power to get the little girl for him."

My dad pinched his chin. "Who sent the dagger with my DNA to the council's headquarters?"

"Edmund," Nicki said. "He had some leftover blood of yours and came up with a plan to get you out of the picture. So he could get his daughter."

"He doesn't know where she is," Dad said.

"But he does know her mother," Nicki said. "And with you out of the picture, Rachel would be more vulnerable."

I'd been wrong to think Edmund wanted my father out of the picture to gain power.

"Son of a bitch," Dad barked. "So Rachel does know where Edmund is. He lured her to him."

"Where's Abbey?" I asked.

"With Olivia," Webb said. "Nicki, where is Edmund's operation in Alaska?"

"With the help of the government, Edmund and Patrick built a large-scale lab in an abandoned warehouse not far from the airport in Anchorage."

The door creaked open. Tripp ambled in, dressed in his black cargo uniform that oozed badass power. A dagger was strapped to each leg, muscles bulged beneath a tight-fitting T-shirt, and a ponytail was tied at his nape. "Mr. Jackson is awake."

"Tripp, take Nicki back to her cell," Dad said.

After unlocking her from the chair, Tripp tied her arms behind her back with a set of cobalt cuffs. Then he gripped her arm. Her eyelids grew heavy. I knew that feeling of weightlessness that occurred every time Tripp touched me with his valium-induced touch.

"Wait." I hopped up. "Nicki, why would you kill someone you love?" I'd read her mind and saw that if she couldn't have Webb, then no one could, but that didn't make sense to me.

Webb wrapped an arm around me.

She set gray eyes on Webb. "Honestly, I loved your sister more. I would have done anything she wanted me to. And she wanted you dead."

As soon as Tripp ushered Nicki out, the three of us sighed. I needed blood. I needed to take a quick catnap, and I needed to hug on Webb for a while.

"Why don't you both see how Mr. Jackson is doing," Dad said. "I have to find Hollings. Considering Nicki's confession, I want to make sure I'm not headed back to Boston. We have much work to do."

"Let's get Crysta to Alaska to do some recon," Webb said. "She's a private detective, and Edmund would never suspect a wolf sniffing around."

"Make it happen." Dad crossed the room. "Oh, and until we settle our score with Edmund, I don't want Nicki's memories of him wiped. We might still need her help." Then Dad was out the door.

"So I guess we can't make out for a week and not get out of bed," I teased.

Webb tunneled his fingers through my hair. "Given what Nicki told us, we will be married sooner than we expected." He delivered his words with surety.

I wanted to suck up all his confidence, but a part of me couldn't. Edmund had slipped through our fingers one too many times.

I peered up at him. "You realize I have to kill Edmund."

He mashed his lips together. "You believe the old man in your dream?"

"Yes. He said I would be the one to kill Edmund."

In my mind, that meant I had to.

12

WEBB

I sat in my office, surfing the multiple web pages on agents Thomas and Wyman. Sawyer had done some digging in the last three days since we had interrogated Nicki. With our security clearances, we had access to top-secret information that we handled within our small SEAL community. However, CIA records weren't ones we could tap into, but Sawyer had mad computer skills. He'd found a back door into the CIA system.

Two pictures showing Thomas and Wyman were lined side by side on my screen. Thomas was a man in his fifties with graying hair and yellow teeth. Wyman, on the other hand, I guessed to be about ten years younger than Thomas with pitch-black hair and even darker eyes. Upon first glance, Wyman could pass for a vampire, but I doubted that any vampires worked for the CIA. The vampire SEAL teams were the only known supernatural beings among the military, at least according to the council of elders. That had been one of my main questions when I'd enlisted in the military. I hadn't broached the subject of supernatural beings until I'd met Steven. And if Steven could convince the top echelon of the human government that a small team of super strong men and women could handle any type of mission, then Edmund could as well.

Our problem wasn't so much the CIA and their knowledge of vampires as it was of our existence leaking out to more humans within the government. We couldn't become lab rats or hunted animals.

Tripp knocked on the doorjamb. "You got a minute?"

I slid my laptop over to the side. "Come in."

Tripp seated himself in one of the two metal chairs that were in front of my desk. "When are you going to clean your office? You've got dust on your shelves ten miles high."

"When my priorities are not trying to keep everyone alive." I didn't care that the bookcases beneath the corner window were covered in dust and who knew what else, or that the pictures of the aircraft carriers and fighter jets hanging on the wall had a film coating the glass frames, or even that the furniture in the small sitting area in the far right corner needed a good cleaning. "Besides, once I retire, this will be your office."

"Pfft. Retire. The elders shot you down once."

I sat back. "The commander is back at the helm. So they have no reason to. But I won't push my retirement until our mission with Edmund is completed. Then I'll submit my recommendation that you fill my spot."

Tripp crossed one leg over the other. "I want to lead, but I thought I would under you. The commander had wanted to get away for a while with Sam and Jo. He has mentioned calling it quits."

Steven hadn't known anything but the military for over thirty or more years. I didn't see how he would be happy. And if he wanted to spend time with his kids, that would have to wait, because Jo and I were not pushing our marriage out any further than we had to, particularly not for her to jet off with her father and brother.

I chewed on the inside of my cheek. "Look, man. I had envisioned getting promoted, but frankly, the political bullshit isn't what

I want. And it's time for me to hand over the reins to someone like you. You're ready."

A strand of Tripp's sandy-blond hair fell out of his leather strap as he leaned forward, resting his elbows on his knees. "Onto the immediate issues. Crysta texted me earlier. She should have information for us in about an hour. She asked that you, me, and the commander be in one room when she calls."

I nodded. "I'm hoping she has some detailed description of what we're up against." We'd sent her to Alaska three days ago, based on the information Nicki had given us.

I pressed the escape button on my laptop, waking up my screen. "I've been reading up on the CIA agents. Thomas is ready to retire. Wyman has been with the CIA for twelve years. But the interesting piece of info I found is that Thomas studied genetics in college alongside Patrick. They were fraternity brothers."

"Well, Kraft and Kodiak are tailing Thomas and Wyman as we speak. They're on their way to Boston. Do you want us to bring them in?"

I tapped my fingers on the desk. "No. I have a better plan. Give Thomas a call and set up a meeting here. That way, we're not raising any red flags if we force them to come in."

Tripp dipped into the side pocket of his cargo pants and pulled out a business card. "What time do you want to meet with them?"

I checked my watch. "See if they can be here at five p.m. That will give us enough time to chat with Crysta."

Tripp straightened. "We could always get both agents into a room and have Sam compel them both. Then they'll tell us what we need to know and even do as we say."

"True, but let's start with a conversation and see what we're dealing with. We also need to determine if Edmund has compelled them already. If that's the case, then we can't." A victim who was under a compelling spell couldn't be compelled by another vampire until the spell had been lifted.

"Where's Jo, by the way?" Tripp asked.

I glanced at my watch. "I'm meeting her in ten minutes in Mr. Jackson's room. She's been helping Dr. Vieira now that Case is behind bars. But she wanted me to talk with Mr. Jackson to gauge whether we can bring him into our circle."

"What are we going to do with Case?"

"Short of killing him, erase his memory. He's a loose cannon. Even when we shut down Edmund and his operation, we can't chance that Case won't side with someone else to expose our existence."

I opened my top side drawer, removed two small vials, and tossed one to Tripp. "Take this. You need to get your system used to the mind-blocking potion before we head into battle." During the last three days, Alia had made up a batch of the potion and given me my own stash. "The effects won't kick in for twenty-four hours, and I want to be ready in the event that we board a plane to Alaska." I'd been handing out vials to our SEAL team only.

"How long will this last?" Tripp asked.

"A good month."

Tripp and I each knocked back the three ounces as though we were doing shots like we had several nights ago.

Twenty minutes later, I was strutting through the infirmary and into Mr. Jackson's room. Ben popped to his feet from the chair on the other side of his father's bed. Jo, who was lounging in the chair near the door, smiled.

My heart opened up so wide when her eyes flashed to violet. Spending an eternity with the vampire beauty was going to be a fantastic ride. "Sorry, I'm late. I can't stay long, either. I have another meeting to get to." The only reason I was even visiting Mr. Jackson was because Jo had wanted me to feel him out to see if we could trust him enough to tell him about Ben and what he had become. But in doing so, we would also expose ourselves, which was not something I was prepared to do, especially given that Mr. Jackson had been a loose cannon as of late with his friends in the Fall River police department.

Regardless, it wasn't out of the question to share our existence with Mr. Jackson. After all, Ben had known about us since he'd walked on base as a human, although I'd put the fear of God into him to keep his mouth shut.

Mr. Jackson appeared rested, clean-shaven, and alert.

"I see you're wide awake," I said.

He squared his shoulders. "And ready to go home with my son." His tone was a little too short for my liking. "Why am I even on the military base? How come I'm not in a hospital in the city?"

Since he'd been compelled by Nicki, I suspected he didn't remember much, although Sam had said Mr. Jackson had been mumbling about Nicki and fangs—another reason to be cautious with him.

"Do you remember anything that happened to you?" Nicki had lifted his spell a few days ago.

"I had a heart attack," he said. "Aside from that, my life has been a blur for the last several months."

Ben winced as his reddish-brown eyes flickered to bright red. "He doesn't remember anything. I've asked him."

I opened up a telepathic connection with Ben. *Ease up on the emotions.*

He shook his close-shaven head and responded with, *Sorry, sir. I'm tired.*

Ben no longer defied me or gave me attitude like he had when he was human and a jealous guy after Jo's love. He'd fought his physical change for months until he showed up on base, asking for our help. I could understand that he wanted a normal life, but what Ben was now was anything but normal, and he had to learn to accept what fate had given him. Unlike us, Ben was a pure human with no natural-born vampire gene. He hadn't had a choice when Edmund injected him with a second-generation batch of vampire serum.

"Ben, why don't you head down to your room and get some sleep," I said. "Your father is in good hands in the infirmary."

"Go, son," Mr. Jackson said. "I'm not leaving."

Ben unfolded his large physique and patted his father on the shoulder. "I'll be back later." Then he sauntered out.

I moved to Ben's spot, only I didn't sit. "Your son has been a great asset to our team. He's going to make a fine soldier when he's done with boot camp."

I stole a look at Jo, who was as beautiful as ever with her long black hair tied back in a braid, her cheeks flushed, her smile stunning. *I love you*, I said to her telepathically.

Her smile grew to large proportions, causing my insides to spark to life.

"Thank you, Lieutenant," Mr. Jackson said. "I would like to spend some time with my son before he resumes his training."

"I'm sure we can arrange to give Ben some leave," I said. "But it might be a couple weeks before we can let him go." If we had to trek to Alaska, then we would need Ben to be part of that mission. His strength alone would serve us well.

"That's okay. It will give me time to take care of some things regarding my mother's death."

I cupped my hands in front of me. "I'm so sorry for your loss." His mother's heart had stopped suddenly at Nicki's hands. Nicki had scared the ninety-year-old woman to death. "I need to run, but if you need anything, do let us know." I crossed the room to Jo. "Can I see you for a minute?"

"Mr. Jackson, I'll be back later," she said.

We closed the door on our way out. "What does he remember?" I asked.

She batted silver eyes at me. "I read his mind. He remembers finding his mother dead, the funeral home, and the fire. Then waking up here." She bit her lip. "We need to tell him what Ben is. Mr. Jackson is too astute not to see the changes in Ben. I want Ben to be happy. And he won't be unless he has his father in his life."

"Can we table Mr. Jackson for now? We have a call with Crysta in about ten minutes."

"Did she find Edmund?" Jo's voice hitched.

"Let's go find out."

Jo and I navigated the halls of the main military compound, where the heart of all action took place. Offices, meeting rooms, the lab-infirmary, the mess hall, the control room, and the barracks made up the four-story building.

"Are you feeling okay?" I asked.

Since she'd read Nicki's mind, Jo had resurrected her past demons, and that had zapped the wind right out of her. She'd been quiet and withdrawn, and she didn't want to talk about what she'd seen in Nicki's memories or what was going on in her own head. I suspected she'd thought of her asshole of a foster dad, who had taken it upon himself to try to have his way with her. The end result —she'd been stabbed twice by him. I'd always promised myself I would kill the guy, but he was human, and Jo didn't need to relive what had happened.

We passed the elevators, making our way to the exit sign and the stairs. I needed to keep moving and not sit idle, or else I would fall asleep. The last three nights, Jo had slept in her room in her father's apartment, while I'd slept in my bed at my quarters on base. Needless to say, without Jo in my arms, I couldn't catch an hour of shut-eye. Then again, I was damned if she was in my arms all night because then I wouldn't get any sleep anyway.

"Why did my dad let Jonah escape with him?" Jo asked.

Steven had gotten a release from the elders since Nicki had confessed. Jonah, on the other hand, hadn't been so lucky. Steven had protested, wanting Jonah to remain on base, but the elders had been steadfast in abiding by vampire laws. I'd been relieved. I didn't trust Jonah, no matter how much Steven read his mind or how much he trusted Jonah. We didn't have time for an enemy to jump ship and join us.

"I suspect it was your father's way of testing Jonah. But it's a moot point now."

She stopped on the fourth floor landing. "So my dad isn't getting his hand slapped for escaping custody?" Her voice echoed.

I snaked an arm around her until my hand was seated in the curve of her lower back. "Sounds to me like you want your dad back in jail."

She angled her head, exposing her creamy neck and carotid artery that was pumping furiously. My fangs dropped as she pressed her chest into me. I lowered my head until my canines were grazing her neck. My body hummed and tightened, while my throat burned to take a sip of her blood.

She moaned as I licked a path from her neck to her ear.

"We can't," I whispered in a voice that was familiar yet foreign.

She slipped her hand in between us, rubbing me everywhere. But when she lingered on my groin, the stairwell darkened. I pushed her up against the wall and was about to sink my fangs into her when my phone trilled, freezing me as the sound pierced my eardrums. I eased back, or more like wobbled, before I checked my phone. A text from Tripp read, *Crysta will call in five minutes.*

Jo heaved a breath, her cheeks pink, her eyelids hooded.

I rubbed my chin, thinking of sea turtles and otters so my cargo pants would loosen. Suddenly, I was glad we hadn't slept in the same bed for the last three nights. My resolve was close to breaking, and at any moment, we would be naked, entwined, and making love for weeks.

13

JO

Webb and I made it from the stairwell to Dad's office in the control room. With all the foreplay he and I had been doing for the last month or more, I was surprised Webb hadn't caved on his promise not to make love to me until we were married. But I smiled, knowing we were closer to taking out Edmund, which meant our wedding was closer. Lately, all I could think about was a Christmas wedding. I thought it would be beautiful to get married amid red and white poinsettias, Christmas trees, lights of all colors, and in a room filled with family and friends. If I wanted that wish to come true, then we had about five weeks to kill Edmund.

The desk phone rang, jolting me back to reality.

Dad pushed a button on the phone, which sat atop a metal desk separating Tripp and me from Webb and Dad.

"Go," Dad said.

"So who is in the room?" Crysta asked.

"The commander, Webb, Jo, and myself," Tripp said.

Normally, the entire SEAL team would be part of the meeting, but Kraft and Kodiak were out on a small job. Sam was in the training room, working with Matthew, and Olivia was stuck with babysitting Abbey, although she'd told me that she'd been enjoying the little girl and the distraction from war, death, and Edmund. I couldn't blame her. With Dr. Case in a jail cell, I'd been helping Dr. Vieira nonstop with targeting a dosage for the antidote.

Crysta cleared her throat. "Here's what you're up against. The warehouse is two or three football fields in size. A high security fence secures the compound. You know, like the ones that you find around prisons. There's been minimal activity up until today. Several truckloads of new humans were brought in and off-loaded. I did see Patrick Mason but not Edmund. I'm trying to get blueprints of the place. I have a buddy in Anchorage who can help me get access to the city planner's office."

Webb's focus was on the phone as though the piece of technology held the magical recipe for shutting down Edmund and his operation. "What about access points?"

"Two gates in and out. Guards are all over the place—outside the perimeter, inside the perimeter, and on the rooftop. I won't know how many doors go into the building until I can see the plans. I could only scope out three sides. The fourth butts up to a mountainside, almost as if the building is tucked into it."

"Are the guards human or vampire?" Tripp asked.

"Both, according to the cool glasses you gave me that distinguish a human's body temperature from a vampire's. However, the human guards are only on the rooftops. I'll have more information tomorrow when I get my hands on the blueprints. I would start planning your mission. In fact, if I were you, I would blow that warehouse to pieces. Take everything out in one shot. Anyway, if you don't have any questions, I'm going to sign off."

"Crysta," I said. "What type of weapons are the guards carrying?" We needed to know if they were armed with guns that shot the bullets filled with the sedative. If that wasn't the case, then Dr. Vieira and I didn't need to worry too much about the antidote.

"I'll double-check tomorrow," she said.

Dad leaned slightly over the desk, his mouth closer to the speaker. "One more thing. Any sign of Rachel?"

"No, sir. But I'll check with my contact. This isn't that big of a city, and locals know when new faces are in town."

"Be careful, cousin," Tripp added. "Edmund could have a slew of locals working for him."

"Got it. Talk soon." Then the phone went dead.

For two beats, no one said anything. I imagined the three of them were calculating a plan. As for me, I didn't know what to say. I was on board with following their orders unless they wanted me to stay away from Edmund, which I couldn't do. He would die by my hand, no matter the consequences.

Dad moved toward the door. "We've got a lot of planning to do. Tripp, get two men and take inventory of the weapons. Webb, get a large map up in the war room and also a head count on soldiers available. That includes the other SEAL team as well."

"Sir," Tripp said to Dad. "Agent Thomas and Wyman will be here in two hours."

"I can read their minds," I said.

Dad gripped the doorjamb. "We need to do this by the book. We're dealing with humans and their government. We don't know what they know. Edmund and Patrick could've prepared them for our supernatural powers. Besides, we need to follow our vampire laws and not reveal what we are to humans, especially the CIA. I would like to stay out of jail."

Webb kissed me on the head. "See you later." Then he and Tripp left.

"I have to run up to the apartment," Dad said. "I forgot my phone."

"I'll go with you." I'd been wanting to talk to Dad about Mr. Jackson and about my dream. With everything going on, I'd barely had time to see Webb, Sam, or Dad.

After a two-minute trek from the control room up to the fourth floor, Dad and I were in the open-plan apartment—a massive room that blended the living area with the kitchen. While Dad disappeared into his room that was tucked away down a short hall, I ventured over to the expansive wall of windows, standing in the path of the sun's rays that spilled in. I closed my eyes, feeling the warmth of the sun and relishing the calm before whatever storm lay ahead.

"Are you ready for that storm?" Dad asked.

I flinched. I didn't even hear him come back. "I'm ready for a life without running, fighting, and always looking over my shoulder. So yeah, I'm ready."

He sat down on an ottoman in front of the oversized chair and tied his boot.

I moseyed over and eased down on the sofa adjacent to him. "Dad? Will you allow Ben to explain to his dad what he is?" Webb had gauged Mr. Jackson's overall demeanor but hadn't spent enough time with Mr. Jackson to tell if we could trust him. "I know we have laws, but Ben wants a relationship with his dad, and Mr. Jackson should know what his son is."

Dad straightened. "Pumpkin, we have too many other things to worry about right now. And I'm not sure telling Mr. Jackson what Ben is is the smartest thing to do. Let me think about it. I would also have to run it by the council."

I played with the seam on the leg of my jeans.

"What else is on your mind?" He chuckled. "I'm seeing an empty brain right now."

I laughed. "In my dream, your dad said I would be the one to kill Edmund. Do you believe he's right?" Deep down, I knew my grandfather spoke the truth. But I wanted validation from someone who was alive and not in my dreams. "Do you also believe what he said about Abbey is true too?"

His green eyes searched mine. "My dad always had an ability to see into the future. He knew you and Sam would be powerful. He knew when you would be born. He even knew that your mom wouldn't live long enough to see you and Sam grow up. So, yes, I do believe him, although I don't want you to fight Edmund."

Silence ticked by as I waited for an onslaught of all the reasons why Dad wasn't going to let me fight. But when second after second passed, it became clear that he would support me.

Dad's phone rang. "Rachel," he said, "where are you?"

"How's Abbey?" Rachel's voice held fear and sadness.

Dad walked over to the window. "Abbey is safe. Tell me where you are."

Rachel sniffled. "I can't."

"Hello, Steven," Edmund said.

I flew off the sofa to stand next to Dad.

The furniture in the room began to shake as Dad's face reddened.

I grasped his wrist, shaking my head, then mouthed, "Calm down."

He inhaled then exhaled slowly. "Edmund, you know you're not getting your daughter."

"Oh, I will, because I'm sure you don't want me to kill Rachel."

"Don't listen to him, Steven," Rachel yelled. "I'll die before I let him have Abbey."

Dad's fangs lowered as his nostrils flared.

"Your silence says you'll listen," Edmund said. "So if you want to see Kraft and Kodiak again, then you will comply with my request."

Dad wrenched a hand through his black hair, silver banishing the green in his eyes. "Bullshit. No way you have my men."

Edmund belted out a sickening laugh. "I'll send you proof." The line went dead.

Tension, fury, and rage—soupy, thick, and suffocating—poured off Dad. Even though I wasn't an empath, every one of his emotions strangled me.

Dad stormed out faster than a 747 airplane at top speed.

For a split second, I didn't know what to do, then the door

slammed so hard that glass shattered from somewhere in the kitchen. Nimble and fast, I darted out of the apartment and into an empty hall. I had no idea where my father had gone, but I knew he wouldn't do something as stupid as exchange Abbey for his men. I sprinted through the halls, down the stairs, and into the control room. I ran by desk after desk until I was in the doorway of my dad's office. But it was empty.

"What's wrong?" Sawyer asked.

I turned toward the vampire with kaleidoscope-colored eyes. "Have you seen my father?"

"No. He left with you," Sawyer said.

I hurried out and checked the war room. Empty. I navigated every office on the second floor, even Webb's. Empty. I did the same on the third floor. No Dad.

I called Dad's phone. It rang until the line clicked to voice mail. I hung up and darted down to the basement. As I did, I called Webb. The line rang and rang. *Argh!* I was about to head to the training room to tell Sam what was going on, when I heard voices coming from the opposite end of the hall where the weapons room was located.

"Commander," Tripp said. "What are you doing?"

I rushed into the weapons room to find Dad collecting daggers, stars, swords, and a gun. I caught his arm. "Dad, stop."

Black threaded through Tripp's bronze eyes. "What happened?"

My dad growled, the sound downright scary, as the guns and daggers on the table before us started dropping to the floor or flying across the room.

I stomped my foot on the tiled floor to let the elemental energy of the earth fill me. Then I sucked in all the air in the room as Tripp grabbed onto his neck, unable to get a breath.

"Get out," I said to Tripp.

He obeyed faster than a speeding train.

My dad hardly felt my wrath like Tripp had. Then again, he was as powerful as me. He didn't stop in his quest to pack weapons into a duffel bag.

I tried again to squeeze the air from his lungs, not to hurt him, but to weaken him so he would stop. But the more I sucked the air out of the room, the faster every dagger and star in the room flew around us, swirling like a tornado.

If Dad wanted to play, then I would. I fisted my hands at my side and concentrated on each dagger until they were all pointing at him. Then I moved so I was facing him. I lifted my arms up and out. "Dad, please stop and talk."

"No," he said in a voice I didn't recognize. "Edmund will die."

"I don't want to hurt you, Dad."

The muscles in my arms were taut, holding the daggers steady, ready to stop my dad.

"You can't hurt me."

The door flew open. Before Dad or I could react, Webb tackled Dad to the floor. The daggers clanked and rolled, while the stars Dad had been holding in midair embedded in the far wall.

Dad shoved Webb off him. "None of you are stopping me."

Both men brushed themselves off as they stood.

Webb glanced at my dad. "What are you talking about?"

"Edmund has Kraft and Kodiak," Dad said.

Webb reared back. "Impossible. They were trailing Agent Thomas and Wyman." He looked at his watch. "Kraft and Kodiak should be back any minute." Webb rushed over to the doorway. "Tripp, call Kraft or Kodiak. See where they are."

My dad's eyes were wild, his fangs dripping with saliva.

I touched his wrist. "Dad, I'm sorry." I was. The last thing I would ever do was hurt my father. "You can't just fly off the handle. Aren't you the one who taught me and your men to think before you act? You always said anger wouldn't get me anywhere. You've counseled Sam on his anger issues a hundred times."

Dad sighed as he briefly closed his eyes. "Edmund will kill Rachel, Kraft, and Kodiak. I can't let that happen."

"Edmund has Rachel too?" Webb asked.

Tripp stuck his head in. "No answer on either Kraft or Kodiak's phone."

Dad's phone rang. He plucked it from his pants pocket. After a swipe, he growled. Then he set the phone down on the table. "There's your answer."

Webb, Tripp, and I glanced at the screen.

I gasped. Tripp and Webb swore.

Kodiak was chained to a wall. Kraft was laid out on the floor, either dead or unconscious. The words under the photo read, *We'll be in touch.*

"How did this happen?" Webb asked no one in particular. "They were tailing the CIA men. Surely, the humans didn't capture them. They don't have the strength."

"They don't need strength," I said. "They just need the bullets filled with the sedative." Dr. Vieira and I had no time left to tweak the antidote. We would have to make a batch no matter if the antidote worked for five minutes or an hour.

WEBB

The CIA agents weren't due to arrive for another hour. After Steven was calm, he and Jo went up to the mess hall to talk. When Tripp had called to tell me the commander and Jo were fighting in the weapons room, I hadn't thought anything of it. Steven and Jo had had a tumultuous relationship; even Sam had fought with Steven on many occasions. But when I'd opened the door to the weapons room, they weren't arguing. It had taken me a minute to react. Jo had had about ten daggers ready to stab her father. Granted, Steven was stubborn and hadn't been listening to her, according to Tripp. Steven had to have been out of control for Jo to do something like stab her own father, although not one blade was pointing at his heart.

"That was weak," Sam said from the other side of the punching bag.

I had to blow off some steam before I met with the agents. My mind was all over the place. My temper was teetering on the edge, much like Steven's, and I itched to kill.

"Get on the mat," Sam ordered, sweat dripping down his face as his five-o'clock shadow colored his angular jaw.

I glared, mainly out of sheer amazement that Sam had turned into a tall, imposing vampire overnight.

"What? I'm not afraid of you, London."

I smoothed a hand over my head. "I am your superior officer." It felt like yesterday that we'd rescued him from Edmund.

Rolling his eyes, Sam crossed the carpeted floor to the thick mat in the middle of the padded room. "In here, you're my underling."

I chuckled. The young vampire had grown some balls. Then again, Sam had always had the fortitude to take control.

"I know you're dying to use your fists on bone and not a punching bag," he said.

I grinned as I met him in the center. "Are you sure you can handle me?"

He let out a laugh.

Before I knew what was happening, Sam whirled around with a roundhouse kick to my jaw. My head went left then back. I touched my jaw before snapping it back into place.

For the next twenty minutes, we danced, punched, kicked, and wrestled. The entire session was freeing and energizing. I had to train more before we headed out to Alaska.

Sam snatched two towels off the chair near the door after we'd finished and threw me one. "So have you decided where the wedding will be?"

"Jo and I haven't talked about it." I wasn't sure why, either. But I made a mental note to broach the topic when she and I were alone. "How is Matthew coming along, and Ben for that matter?"

Sam wiped his face. "Ben is doing great. Matthew has a long way to go."

"We'll need Ben for the upcoming mission. I was hoping we could use Matthew, too, now that Kraft and Kodiak have been captured."

"Use his grandfather, Victor," Sam said. "He helped you when you came to rescue Jo and me from the funeral home."

I toweled the sweat off my neck. "Great idea." Victor could wield a sword better than anyone.

"Webb, can I sit in on your meeting with those human agents? I know I'm not an official SEAL yet, but I want to learn as much as I can."

He did have strong empath abilities that could detect if the humans were lying or scared, although it was easy to detect fear in humans just by their scent.

"With Kraft and Kodiak out and Olivia guarding Abbey, I could use your help. But I don't want to overwhelm the two agents with a room full of people. Let me check with your dad on how we want to handle the meeting."

He nodded. "I'm going to head up to the apartment and clean up. Text me."

He collected his bag, and we both left. I ran up to the men's barracks on the third floor. After a quick shower, I dressed in a fresh uniform and sent Steven a text. *Let's talk before the agents arrive. I'll be in my office.*

I'll be there in one minute, he responded.

We had ten minutes before the agents showed.

When I walked into my office, Steven was engrossed in his phone.

I skirted by him to sit in my chair. "Has Edmund sent another text?"

He set his phone in his lap. "No. And before you ask, my daughter is in the lab with Dr. Vieira, helping him with the antidote. She'll not be joining us for the meeting." His tone was resolute and laced with lingering anger.

I was always thinking of Jo, but she didn't need to be in the meeting. "You're still pissed, I see." I didn't need him to meet with the human agents while he was in a mood that would scare them into leaving. "We need to be even-tempered as we plan and keep the endgame in perspective. Kraft and Kodiak will be fine. Edmund isn't going to do anything to them, not if he's trading them for Abbey."

"It's Rachel I'm worried about," Steven said.

"I am too." Boy, was I. I didn't want to see Abbey grow up without her mom.

Steven pinched the bridge of his nose. "I saw stars when Edmund said he had Kraft and Kodiak. But you're right. Jo said the same thing to me when we were in the mess hall."

"Did you two work things out?" I asked.

"Yeah. She was just trying to stop me from doing something stupid. I saw firsthand how powerful she really is."

I thought for a second, trying to remember if Steven had ever seen Jo in action, and I couldn't recall one time he had. I'd seen her power when she and Sam had worked together to stop the vampires from entering that cabin in Alaska.

"We have about two minutes before the agents are here," Steven said. "How do you want to play this?"

"You and I will meet with them in the viewing room off the lobby that has the hidden cameras. Tripp and Sam will be positioned in the room next door, watching everything from the monitors."

"Good plan. And their background?"

I'd told Tripp but hadn't filled in the commander. "You'll love this. Agent Thomas and your brother, Patrick, were fraternity brothers in college. In fact, Thomas studied genetics."

He cocked an eyebrow. "This will be an interesting meeting for sure." Steven's phone buzzed. "Yes, Ruth? Make them comfortable in the viewing room. We'll be right down." He hung up. "Show time."

Before we left, I texted Tripp and Sam to get settled into the computer room in the lobby. Then we made our way down. I prayed that Steven and I could keep our wits about us and not kill the humans. Given Steven's outrage earlier, I had the better chance of not taking off the humans' heads, but we were both ready to explode.

The lobby was cold and sterile, like always. A circular desk surrounded Ruth, our receptionist, who appeared as though she was down in a hole with only her blond head visible.

I checked on Tripp and Sam. "You guys ready?"

Tripp pushed in a button on the twenty-inch computer screen that hung on the wall separating the computer room from the viewing room. "We will be in a second."

Sam slid into a chair next to Tripp. "This should be fun."

"If things get out of hand," I said, "get in there."

They both gave me a thumbs-up.

Steven waited for me before we entered the viewing room. When we did, both agents hopped up. With introductions out of the way, Agent Thomas, who had graying hair and yellow teeth, sat in one of the four chairs around the square table. Like the room Jo and I had spoken to Steven in at vampire headquarters, this room was bare bones with no windows.

Agent Wyman, who had slicked-back hair and black-as-night eyes, sat next to his partner, while Steven and I filled the remaining two chairs across from the humans.

"I understand," Steven said, "that Agent Thomas has been here on base once already. You have questions?"

Thomas nodded. "I do. Our office was brought in on the lab explosion case that happened last month on the Indian reservation. Our boss wanted to make sure the explosion was not terrorist-related. Anyway, the coroner found some abnormal bone structure on three of the victims."

"And abnormalities on the victims scream terrorist?" I asked. "Also how did the trail lead you to us?"

Short of Edmund sending these two yahoos to us, there was no evidence to show that my unit had anything to do with the incident.

The agents gave each other a smug look.

Wyman leaned his elbows on the table. "We found a car at the scene that belonged to a Howell Gonzalez. He told us to check with the folks at the military base in town."

I deadpanned, while inside I was ready to use whatever scare tactics I could to get them to come clean. Regardless, I didn't believe for a second that Howell had sent these agents our way. The vampire wanted to help us, not start trouble. Besides, I'd saved his life. Surely, he didn't want to die so soon.

"Let's drop the bullshit," I said. "What is it that you're really after?" I flared my nostrils, sniffing the humans, but detected no signs of fear. Edmund had prepared them.

Thomas sat back as though he was the one who held all the cards. "I'm not sure what you're getting at. We're here doing our job. Nothing more."

"I'll be frank," Steven said. "As the commander and officer in charge of this base and the SEAL teams, I have access to top-secret information. And I am not aware of any job by the CIA to investigate a local fire. I'm also aware, Agent Thomas, that you're in possession of a collection of blood samples that were supposed to be sent to our lab in Boston. Now tell me, why would you need blood samples from this base? Because the way I see it, I can detain you for stealing top-secret data."

Thomas arched his back. "I've done no such thing. Besides, you can't prove that."

I moved in my seat. "Are you that dumb to think that we don't have proof?"

"Or that we don't know, Agent Thomas, that you are working with my brother, Patrick?" Steven asked.

Silence whipped around like an icy wind on the North Atlantic in the dead of winter.

Agent Thomas kicked back his chair before he slapped his hand down on the table. The sound boomed, almost hurting my eardrums. "I know what you two are." He wagged a finger between Steven and me.

Steven schooled his anger, which I could feel dripping off him. "And what is that?"

Wyman watched quietly as though he was enjoying the interaction.

Thomas leaned over slightly, his cigarette breath potent as he bared his yellow teeth. "You're not human."

Steven and I laughed.

"Don't mock me," Agent Thomas said.

"Wyman, do you agree with your partner?" I asked.

All eyes went to the dark-haired agent.

"I know that the bodies that were uncovered at the lab explosion weren't normal." He sounded like a robot.

"So are you also under orders from your CIA director to kidnap my men?" Steven asked.

Wyman and Thomas exchanged a surprised look.

I angled my head at both agents. "Yeah, you two are guilty." I craned my neck up at the light. "Tripp, send in the guards."

"Wait," Wyman said. "You can't arrest us. You're not even the law."

Steven rose as though a spirit had lifted him from the grave. He slowly pressed his hands on the table, swinging his gaze between the agents.

Agent Thomas inched back as a rancid smell of body odor permeated the stuffy air.

Steven bent over slightly. "You are stupid." Each word was delivered with a precise tone devoid of feeling. "The minute you drive through my gate on government property, CIA or not, you abide by my rules. And if you don't start talking, I'll see to it that neither of you walk out of here."

Wyman did a double take. Thomas gaped.

Sam and Tripp entered.

Wyman and Thomas paled as they laid eyes on Sam and Tripp.

We were all tall, broad, and scary compared to the agents, who were a good head shorter than us.

"We'll take care of them." Sam wet his lips as though he wanted to sink his fangs into them. I would guess he did. Human blood, no matter how rancid the scent of fear was, did taste good.

"You can count on us to get answers," Tripp chimed in.

"Throw them in a cell," Steven ordered.

Tripp handcuffed Thomas, while Sam did the same to Wyman. Both agents jerked and kicked, but they were no match for the strength of Sam and Tripp.

"You'll pay for this," Thomas said.

"I got a family," Wyman whined, a distinct change from his earlier cocky tone. "Can I at least call them?"

I have an idea, I said to Steven via a telepathic connection.

Steven dipped his chin.

"Tripp," I said. "Take Agent Thomas. Sam will follow with Wyman in a second."

Thomas struggled to get free. "Wyman, keep your mouth shut."

Tripp shoved Thomas out of the door.

I pushed to my feet, staring at Wyman. "I'll make you a deal. You tell us what we want to know, and we'll let you call your family." It was time to unleash our supernatural powers, vampire laws be damned. I was tired of dancing around.

Wyman considered all of us in the room.

Sam, who had a death grip on Wyman's arm, let go. "Dude, you have a choice here. Make the right one."

Wyman bowed his head. "I'll cooperate, provided I can walk out of here."

I opened a telepathic connection to Steven. *If we let him walk, then we'll need to erase his memories of everything he knows about us. It goes against your by-the-book rule, but we don't have time to dick around.*

I agree, he responded.

"It's a deal," I said. "Start from the beginning."

Wyman dropped into the chair. "Agent Thomas has been working with his buddy from college, Patrick Mason, your brother." He regarded Steven. "Patrick wants to sell his genetic research to the government. He claims he can build super soldiers, as in people who can take out our enemies. At first, Thomas and I didn't believe Patrick until he showed us a video of a man's ability before he injected him with some type of serum and after. But we were still skeptical. So Patrick invited us to his research facility in Anchorage. It was there that we couldn't believe our eyes. He's got a warehouse full of recruits who are amazingly strong and incredibly scary."

Steven sighed. "And what's your purpose for snooping around here?"

"Patrick wanted us to find a little girl and bring her to him. If we did, he would show us more of his research."

Steven pressed his lips tightly together. Sam had a blank expression on his face as he stood guard next to Wyman.

"And my men?" I asked.

Lines creased Wyman's forehead. "I don't know anything about your men. I swear."

"Does Patrick have any men in the city?" Sam asked.

"We met with a man earlier today named Dyson. He said he was with a government office in Boston and working with Patrick."

Son of a bitch. Dyson was also Elder Dyson, as in Hollings's colleague.

I gave Steven a sidelong glance. "That explains a lot." *More than a lot.* I wondered if Hollings knew, and I was also curious what Dyson's motivation could be. If I had to guess, I would say money. Greed and power were strong incentives to go against the law.

Steven didn't show any signs of rage. Instead, he spoke in a calm voice. "Does Dyson have dark hair with a gray streak that stands out on his left side?"

Wyman nodded.

I gripped the back of the chair. "Two more questions. Who else within your organization knows about Patrick's research? And what did Thomas do with the blood samples that he took from here?"

Wyman rubbed his thumbs together, a nervous tick no doubt. "Since Patrick isn't ready to roll out his entire research, Thomas and

I haven't taken the info up our chain of command. We have to have more than some strong men and women to prove that they pass as super soldiers. As far as the blood samples, we gave them to Dyson."

I blew out a quiet breath, knowing our DNA hadn't fallen into the hands of the human government.

Steven popped off the wall. "Here's what you're going to do. When you leave here, you'll take your family and disappear. No contact with your employer or Agent Thomas or anyone other than your family. Is that understood?"

Wyman nodded vigorously.

I eyed Sam as I spoke to him telepathically. *Erase his memories of this conversation and everything he's seen with Patrick. Then compel him to get out of town with his family and not to speak to anyone within the CIA, Edmund's organization, or Dyson.*

Sam blinked.

I moved toward the door. "Agent Wyman, Sam will escort you out. Thank you for cooperating. What you've told us will save lives."

Wyman smiled.

Steven followed me out. As soon as we were in the elevator, Steven punched the wall, putting a deep dent into the metal structure. I stabbed the button for the fourth floor. I had to see Jo. She was the only one who could take me to a quiet place, which I needed so desperately at the moment. Otherwise, I would also be punching something, and I needed my strength for the real fight. I had no idea how we would handle the news of Dyson being a mole, although if it were up to me, I would hunt him down right now and kill him.

The elevator doors opened.

Steven and I stepped out.

"We both need to take a breather before we regroup," I said. My head was spinning, and I would bet his was too.

Steven flicked a thumb behind him. "I'm going to check on Olivia and Abbey. They're in my apartment. I'll also contact Hollings, tell him the news, and get him back here."

"With Kraft and Kodiak detained, we need more troops. I'll call Victor Costner." I checked my watch. "How about midnight in the war room?" That would give us six hours to call in folks, relax, and think straight.

He nodded as he ambled down the hall to his apartment.

I went in the opposite direction. It was time to steal my future bride for some quiet time.

15

WEBB

Jo and I were snuggled up on the couch at my house on base. Beethoven's Piano Quartet in E-flat Major was playing on repeat in the background. I wasn't much into music, but I did love some of the classical pieces, which relaxed and calmed me.

My legs were kicked out on top of the coffee table, while Jo snored lightly with her head in my lap. She'd been sleeping for the last four hours. I'd closed my eyes for about two hours. Now I was staring at the picture directly ahead of me that portrayed a beautiful sunrise over the Atlantic. I'd taken that photo the morning after I moved into my house in Maine over four years ago. That day had been one of the most peaceful days in my entire life. The water had been like glass with the waves sweeping the shore as gracefully as a ballet dancer, while the sun peeked over the horizon, casting a soft glow across the sky. I wanted that day back again. I wanted Jo to experience the beauty of nature and the peace that nature had to offer.

Soon enough, I told myself as I began to trace the outline of her ear.

She stirred in my lap before she sat up and yawned. "We're just a lively couple, aren't we?"

"We needed the rest," I said.

She adjusted, turning over on her back with her head still in my lap. "I can't read your mind. You've taken that mind-blocking potion."

I tapped her on the nose. "Didn't we talk about you staying out of my mind?"

She sighed. "You've been preoccupied, and I want to make sure you're okay."

"You almost died," I said. "And I can't seem to get that out of my head, especially not when we're about to confront Edmund. I'm tired of worrying about you getting killed."

She found my hand that was lying on her stomach and started rubbing my fingers. "I'm sorry about not being more attentive when I was near Nicki at the funeral home. She just made me so angry."

"Anger can be good and bad," I said. "Around your enemy, you have to temper that anger to be able to think on a dime. Promise me you'll be more prepared when we face off with Edmund." I knew better than anyone that rage could fuck up a mission in less than a second. Edmund was a prime example, considering he'd lost all thought when he killed Ella Case.

"I promise," she said with conviction. "Was that all you were thinking about?"

I dragged my hand through her hair as I grinned. "No. I was daydreaming about us, about how I can't wait to get married. Speaking of marriage, we haven't talked about where we would get married. Any ideas?"

She sighed as she glanced at the window area. "I have been thinking. What if we get married next month around Christmas? Of course, it would be too cold for a beach wedding in December. I know that's one place you wanted to get married."

"The beach would be nice in the summertime. Frankly, I don't care if it's a beach, a church, or any place as long as we get married.

But why Christmastime?" Not that I was complaining. I loved the idea.

She gnawed on her bottom lip. "Growing up, Sam and I never had a true Christmas. We hardly got presents from our foster families. Most of them couldn't afford to spend a lot of money, especially with their own kids. And I've never experienced the true meaning of Christmas with a family who loves me. I know I had Sam, but we didn't have our parents. So it would mean so much to me to celebrate our marriage on that day with my dad there and all my other extended family, like Olivia and the SEAL team."

As she was talking, I couldn't help but think of Victor Costner's large estate, where he'd held the charity ball last spring. That would be a perfect venue. "What would you think about asking Victor if we could get married on his estate? He'll be here for the meeting. We can ask him then."

Her silver eyes widened. "Oh my God. That would be perfect." Then she frowned. "But what if we can't get Edmund out of our lives before then."

"Then we adapt. We can always get married on the beach behind my house in Maine in the spring." Not that I wanted to wait that long, but I would if our mission wasn't successful.

She laughed. "If we have to wait until the spring then I want you to make love to me on Christmas. I'm not waiting longer than that. Deal?"

The silky strands of her hair slipped through my fingers. Before I could say a word, she straddled my lap and shoved her tongue in my mouth.

I chuckled.

She nibbled on my lips. "Don't say no. Just think about it."

That was all I thought about.

She peppered kisses all over my face. I leaned my head back against the couch and let her explore and have her way as a slow fire started, igniting the tingling sensation coursing through my body.

The tips of her canines grazed my neck before she bit, quick and deep.

I almost shot off the couch. Instead, I stilled, listening to her moan, moving her sweet hips as she pressed her body against mine. I was in heaven with an inferno blazing inside me. I angled my neck, giving her better access to take as much as she needed.

The sound of my phone tore through my haze, but that didn't stop Jo. I considered not answering the call, but I was waiting to hear from George. I'd called him before I fell asleep. Not to mention, if Jo's father was calling and I didn't answer, he might assume the worst. The phone stopped only to start blaring again in the quiet room.

"Jo, I have to answer it."

She tucked her fangs away as she climbed off me and disappeared through the arched doorway into the other part of the house.

I adjusted my groin as I got up and answered my phone. "Hello." My voice was husky.

"Howell should arrive on base within the hour," George said.

"Perfect. Thank you."

"Do you need my help with anything else?" he asked.

"Um, yeah." I stalked over to the arched doorway that Jo had gone through. I didn't see her, so I moved to the window in the living room that faced the front of the house. "That hotel Jo and I stayed at recently in Boston. Can you check their availability for a honeymoon suite for next month?" I kept my voice to a whisper.

"When's the big day?" George asked with pride in his voice.

He was like a father to me.

"Not sure yet, but Jo wants to get married sometime around Christmas."

"What about Edmund?" he asked.

As I stood looking out at the sparse tree limbs, I didn't know if waiting to kill a vampire who wouldn't seem to die was the right thing to do. I couldn't keep putting off my life or Jo's because

Edmund was walking the earth. And whether Edmund was alive or dead, I wanted to marry Jo. I wanted her to be my wife, my everything. Not only that, she was right. She'd said on a few occasions that we might not be here tomorrow. *Fuck.* If her in a coma wasn't enough to wake me up, I didn't know what was.

"Webb?" George's voice cut through my thoughts.

"I'm still here. Regardless if Edmund is alive or dead, Jo and I will get married at Christmas."

"I'm so glad to hear that," George said. "I'll do some homework. Be safe."

The line clicked off.

I hurried through the house, looking for my gorgeous vampire. I found her in the bathroom, brushing her hair, looking beautiful and somewhat rested. I wrapped my arms around her from behind as my lips ghosted over her neck. I dared not bite since her blood was like a fine whiskey, smooth and strong. I needed my wits about me to get through the meeting and beyond.

She melted back into me. "You seem extremely happy all of a sudden."

"I had an epiphany." I locked eyes with her in the mirror. "Whether we kill Edmund before Christmas or not, you and I will get married then."

She sucked in a large amount of air, squealing as she turned in my arms. "Seriously?"

I lifted her up on the sink. "You've always been right. We can't live our lives based on someone else or on what could happen." I swiped my fingers over her rosy cheeks. "We deserve to start our future together."

Her lips locked with mine. I kissed her with all the energy I had, taking as much as I could, memorizing the way her lips molded with mine, the way she tasted of home, sunshine, and my future. I would die before I let anything happen to her.

After that body-humming kiss that lasted a good five minutes, we left the house for the meeting.

The bright lights of the war room made me squint. It took me a second to clear my vision. When I did, Victor Costner; his daughter, Alia; her son, Matthew; and Sam were busy talking to one another.

Jo glided over to Matthew, who was by far not the lanky human anymore. Since turning vampire, his upper torso had broadened and his jaw had grown sharper, much like his grandfather, Victor's. The only attributes of Matthew's that matched his mother's were his blond hair and blue eyes.

I settled next to Victor. The last time I'd seen the formidable vampire was when he had helped Olivia and me find Sam and Jo, and he'd almost taken Edmund's head off. Man, when he'd had Edmund in his grasp, I'd held my breath, praying so damn hard Victor would slice Edmund's head right off. Sadly, Edmund had been quicker.

Victor extended his hand. "Webb, good to see you." He raked his dark gaze over my face. "You look tired."

Story of my life.

After a tight and quick handshake with Victor, I nodded to everyone.

Jo slid next to me. "Victor, while we have a minute, Webb and I would like to ask you a favor. We were wondering if we could get married on your estate next month."

Alia's voice hitched. "Jo, we would be honored to host your wedding."

Victor grinned. "We owe you both for saving Matthew. And as Alia said, we would be honored."

Jo threw her arms around Alia. "Thank you." She went to hug Victor, when the side door opened with a creak.

The air thickened when Sam jerked his head at Howell. "What is *he* doing here?" Sam snarled as black threaded through his green irises.

I jumped in front of Sam. "I called him."

Howell strutted over, his bald head glistening beneath the lights. The last time I'd seen the vampire, his hair was on fire and his skin was falling off him. Now it appeared as though he was a brand-new vampire.

He arched a brow as he set his sights on me. "I look that bad, London?"

"I'm surprised your hair didn't grow back." As vampires, we could heal from just about anything. I was slowly learning that maybe our physical characteristics as vampires didn't render us totally immortal.

He rubbed a hand over his head. "Nah, I shaved it."

Sam sidled up to me with a scowl on his face. "Explain what he's doing here."

I opened my mouth, but Howell held up his hand. "Let me. Look, Sam, I get you're ready to drive a dagger into my heart, but Webb saved my life, and I owe him. I'm not here to give you shit or get into a fight. The only fighting I want to do is kill the asshole who decided to blow up the building I was in."

Sam lowered his shoulders but kept the scowl. "Then maybe my sister should read your mind before we embark on this mission."

That was my plan before we started our meeting. "We'll make that happen," I said.

Suddenly, an eardrum-piercing roar caused the room to shake and sent me running out the side door. I found Steven in the hall with his fist through the wall and his phone pressed to his ear. We had several holes in walls around the base that we would have to fix.

"I will carve you into tiny pieces when I get my hands on you," Steven yelled.

Edmund's voice came through the phone. "I would like to see you try."

Jo, Sam, Alia, Victor, Howell, and Matthew spilled into the hall.

I wrangled them back into the war room. "Let's get settled. Sam, can you call Tripp and Olivia and see where they are? Jo, find Ben, please."

Once they were back inside, I blocked the door while I listened.

Steven hit the speaker button and held out the phone with his fangs down, eyes narrowed, and face beet red.

"Agent Thomas and Wyman seem to be ignoring my calls." Edmund's voice echoed in the hall. "Any idea where they are?"

Steven let out a low, evil chuckle. "The humans are no concern of yours. And tell me, why would you involve the human government in your grand scheme?"

We knew the answer, but I suspected Steven wanted to hear the reason from the horse's mouth.

Jo came out and gently moved me out of the way, or more like I moved of my own accord.

"You know that I've always wanted to take over the world," Edmund said in a condescending tone.

Steven sneered. "The only world you'll be taking over is hell."

Edmund's laughter rumbled through the phone. "Enough of your threats. I want my daughter. A father deserves to see his daughter."

"Don't listen to him, Steven." Rachel's tone was sharp.

Then the sound of him slapping her made Jo, Steven, and I flinch.

"You're a sick creep," Jo said, fisting her hands at her sides.

"My sweet Jo. I'm sad that you haven't contacted me. I truly wanted you to work for me. I see, though, that your father got out of jail. Too bad. I tried everything I could to get him out of the picture." Edmund's tone had changed from snarky to warm. "We could've done great things together."

"Enough," I blurted out. "You will not get your daughter or anyone else."

"Tsk. Tsk. Tsk." Edmund's voice was sharper and more irritating than a high-pitched dog whistle. "Webb, you know better than to spit threats. Let's not forget I have two of your top vampires. I'm sure you don't want to lose two more men. You've already lost three."

I inhaled a deep breath then let it out slowly. He had me by the balls. I couldn't afford to lose Kraft and Kodiak. Between Bruno and Edmund's plans for power and greed, we'd lost Quade, Crowe, and Sloan.

"Your silence tells me that you will listen to my demands," Edmund said.

Rachel sniffled in the background.

Steven chewed on the inside of his cheek. "We know you're in Alaska. We know that Elder Dyson has been working with you. We know Dr. Case has been feeding you and my brother information. We know you killed the Secretary of the Navy. The only logical next step is to kill you."

"Are you saying that you don't want to negotiate to save your men?" Edmund asked.

"You're not getting Abbey," Jo blurted out.

"That's too bad," Edmund responded.

"No, Edmund. Please don't. Steven, you've got to bring my daughter to me," Rachel pleaded.

"It's too late for that, Rachel," Edmund said before Rachel screamed at the top of her lungs.

Then, complete silence.

Jo slapped a hand over her mouth as tears filled her eyes. My heart sank. Steven froze, horror jumping off him.

Edmund clucked his tongue. "If you don't want your men to end up like Rachel, then bring me Abbey, or else I'll not only kill Kodiak and Kraft, but the wolf shifter as well." The line went dead.

I'd heard him when he'd said he had Crysta, but I was stuck on Rachel's demise, although Tripp wouldn't be pleased to hear that his cousin had been captured.

Hollings ran in from the control room, panting. His dark eyes swam with rage and fear. "Dyson took Jonah. They're both gone."

I got whiplash from everything that was happening at once, although Jonah was the least of our concerns. Whether he was on our side or Edmund's, it didn't matter. He would die if he got in my way.

Hollings labored for breath. "What happened?"

Steven pressed his fingers to his temple. "I'll fill you in later. Webb, wheels up in two hours. Get the team ready, including Dr. Vieira. Then call in Viking II. We need all the fighters we can get."

I nodded as I pulled out my phone. Viking II was our other vampire SEAL team, and they were on standby in the event we needed their help.

"Oh my God," Jo said. "I can't believe Rachel is dead. How are we going to tell Abbey?"

Hollings gaped. "You're kidding me. Rachel is dead?"

Steven stormed out. "Come on, Hollings. Let's catch up while I pack up my weapons."

No sooner had they left Jo and me standing in the hall than Olivia walked out of the control room with Abbey in her arms.

The little girl jumped down and ran, her black ponytails swinging and her big blue eyes focused on Jo. She leapt into Jo's arms. "My mommy." Abbey started to cry. "She died."

"How do you know?" Jo asked.

We all knew Abbey had visions, but she could've heard us in the hall too.

Abbey flattened a palm on Jo's face. "I'll show you."

Jo closed her eyes for a long minute before tears streamed down her face. "I'm so sorry." She hugged Abbey to her, while the little girl quietly cried.

I took Abbey in my arms. "We won't let anything happen to you." I rubbed her back as she laid her head on my shoulder.

I didn't know what would happen next, but one thing was certain—Edmund would die soon if for nothing else, taking Abbey's mom away from her.

16

JO

I stared out the window of the plane as I replayed Abbey's vision over and over in my mind. Edmund had driven a dagger straight through Rachel's neck. The scene, along with Abbey's crying, had gutted me. She would never see her mom again.

I closed my eyes, listening to Dad give out orders of what to do when we landed. I should join in the discussion, but I couldn't bring myself to think of anything other than how I would kill Edmund. I still didn't know if I would be the one. I did believe in what my grandfather had said to me in my dream. Maybe that was the reason I didn't care to add my two cents to the discussion.

Webb's woodsy scent announced him before he sank into the seat next to me. "I'm worried about you. Are you up for this?"

The clouds outside the window clipped by.

"I will be," I said in a quiet voice.

Touching my face, Webb guided me to look at him. "I'm all for you sitting this one out. But if your grandfather said you will be the one to end Edmund, then we need you at a hundred percent."

My gaze melded with his. "I'm in. I just needed some time to

137

process what Abbey showed me." I leaned my head on his shoulder. "Is Abbey asleep?"

Webb interlaced his fingers with mine. "She's sound asleep in Alia's lap."

Before we left Massachusetts, Dad and Webb had debated on whether to bring Abbey along. In the end, they hadn't wanted to take any chances on leaving her behind in the event Edmund had someone waiting in the wings to snag her, like Jonah or Dyson.

The plane's engine droned to a quiet hum as I listened to Dad. He wanted to take out every guard on the premises and replace them with our team. That could work, giving us access to get inside, although the mystery was how many more guards and soldiers were inside that warehouse. According to the feedback Crysta had given us before she was captured, she'd seen a truck full of humans. But that had been one truckload. If there were more inside, we could be facing an army of misfit vampires. And if they were anything like Blake Turner, fierce and strong, then we could be walking into a death trap.

I hated to even think that the only surefire way to get in was with Abbey. As much as I didn't want to subject her to Edmund, we desperately needed to assess the inside of his fortress.

I lifted my head. "I have an idea that my dad should hear."

Webb didn't waste any time in getting up. I followed him to the back of the plane. The team was split up on both sides. Abbey had her head in Alia's lap, sleeping. Alia's eyes were closed. Howell and Dr. Vieira were reading on their phones. Victor and his grandson, Matthew, were sitting together, talking. Sam and Ben were playing cards. Olivia and Tripp were crowded in the back galley with my dad, where he had a drawing of Edmund's compound.

Dad stopped talking when I approached. "What is it?"

Webb leaned against the bathroom door, and I settled next to him. "The only way we're going to win against Edmund is if we give him Abbey. And before you say no, hear me out. If Edmund gets Abbey, then he gets me. He did want me to work for him.

Anyway, he'll be preoccupied with Abbey. In the meantime, I can assess what we're up against."

Dad chewed on the inside of his cheek.

Webb's cobalt-blue eyes flashed to vampire black. "If you did go in, how would you get us the information?"

I bit my lip. "I'll find a way. Maybe I can leave a door unlocked. Also, before I go in with Abbey, he has to release Kraft, Kodiak, and Crysta. That was the deal after all. Right? And they might have better information for you on how to get in."

"Storming the place would only drive Edmund to flee," Tripp said. "We do need to catch him off guard. And if we take out his guards and insert ours, then we can use their security credentials to get inside. We'll have the man power to do that with our Viking II SEAL team."

Dad dragged a hand over his unshaven jaw. "We do need Kraft and Kodiak. And we do need to know the ins and outs of that ware-house." Dad pointed to the plans on the counter. "These blueprints aren't telling us much."

Webb's nostrils flared. "I don't like it. I can't lose you again, Jo."

I frowned. I didn't want to die. I wanted to get married, make love to Webb for the first time, have Dad walk me down the aisle. And now that Abbey didn't have a mom, I wanted to be there for her. As a female vampire, I couldn't have kids. So I wanted to be the stand-in mom for her.

"One problem," Dad said. "Your grandfather told you that we need to protect Abbey. Handing her over to Edmund is not protecting her."

"That's why she and I are a package deal. I'll protect her. Besides, Edmund isn't going to harm Abbey." I wasn't sure of that, but he wanted his daughter badly, so he wouldn't do anything to her, at least not right away.

"But he could kill you," Webb added. "Then Abbey won't have anyone to protect her."

I considered Dad and Webb. Both were struggling with my plan, which wasn't surprising. The fact that we were even discussing my plan made me stand up straighter. They believed in me. They believed I could handle myself. I understood their hesitation too.

Olivia, who had been quiet, spoke up. "Edmund has been all talk when it comes to Jo. I don't believe he ever wanted to kill her. As we know, he wanted her DNA and might still. So as far as Jo, I don't believe he will rush to end her life. I also agree that Edmund won't lay a finger on Abbey. He'll be too smitten with her to react in a violent way, at least in the beginning. So that will give us time to regroup and shut him down for good. We do desperately need Kraft and Kodiak's skills. We could use Crysta's talent as a wolf shifter. But the only thing I caution you on"—Olivia fixated on me—"is don't go in with your guns blazing and piss off Edmund. Keep calm. Do as he says. This is all about keeping both Jo and Abbey safe. If we're not inside within twenty-four hours, then find a way to first kill your uncle Patrick. Without him, Edmund can't continue to build a vampire army." She looked at me. "And under no circumstances do you let Abbey out of your sight."

I would do everything in my power not to let anything happen to her. I wished there was a better plan. But storming the warehouse without meeting Edmund's demands would only get us through the door, and more people would get killed. The end result would be the same—Edmund would escape us again. With my plan, it was better to be closer to my enemy. That way if Edmund did disappear with Abbey and me, at least I could do everything in my power to kill him.

"You do bring up all valid points," Dad said to Olivia.

Webb shook his head. "Sometimes, Olivia, I do hate you. But I also respect the way you think."

She rolled her brown eyes. "Jo is tough. She can handle herself."

"True," Webb glanced at me with love and fear. "But I would like to prevent my heart from stopping again. And it will if Jo dies."

I leaned into Webb. "I'm not going to die. I have nine lives. I know I've only used two," I teased.

Webb tensed. "You have got to make sure you have all your senses open. Nothing can happen like it did with Nicki. You must be vigilant in making sure you know the room, the exits, the heartbeats, and the sounds. You took that mind-blocking potion, so he won't be able to read your mind, but you can still read his and anyone else's. Just don't get too deep into their minds, or else you'll tire yourself."

"Jo," Dad said. "I want you to take an extra dose of the antidote before we land. We don't know how long you'll be in there. And if they do shoot you with the sedative, act like the drug works. Then they might leave you alone long enough so you can do some detective work."

I hadn't thought that far ahead, but that was a great idea. Although if I did act as if I was passed out, then I wouldn't have eyes on Abbey. I nodded at Dad, anyway. I would determine my next move as I went along. All the planning in the world was great, but sometimes, plans didn't work out the way they were set.

17

JO

We sat parked in a windowless van about two miles outside of Edmund's compound. The weather was brisk for November in Alaska, and daylight was slowly slipping away. Aside from Dad, Webb, Olivia, Abbey, and me, the rest of the team had checked into a motel somewhere north of where we were.

Abbey was strapped in between Webb and me in the back seat. "Are we ready to see my daddy?" Her voice held a note of sadness. I suspected it wasn't because of Edmund but because her mom was dead.

We had talked to Abbey on the way from the airport, letting her know that she and I would pay a visit to her father. With her visions, she didn't seem surprised.

Webb hung his arm on the back of the seat as he lowered his head to Abbey. "Will you be a brave and strong girl for us and listen to Jo?"

"I'm not afraid," Abbey said in her singsong voice.

"That's my girl," Webb said.

I couldn't be afraid, either. I had a job to do, and that was to keep her safe. I didn't want to die, but I would if it meant giving my life for Abbey's. After all, she was an important part of the vampire world and keeping our existence alive.

Dad studied me from the driver's seat as though he was trying to get into my mind. I was thankful for the mind-blocking potion. I didn't want to give him a reason to worry any more than he already was.

"Are we ready to make the call?" Olivia asked.

Edmund hadn't given us a timeline for delivering Abbey. However, we'd made haste in getting on the plane, which had been fine with me. I was extremely anxious to get past the fighting and get on with my life, but dread filled my stomach.

My dad dialed Edmund's number. The line rang once.

"Have you come to your senses?" Edmund's deep and scratchy voice sent a shiver down my spine. I shouldn't have felt icky about Edmund. My last interaction with him had been quite pleasant at times until he'd learned of Abbey.

"Here's the plan," Dad said. "Jo and Abbey will be outside the gate of your complex in five minutes. Have Kraft, Kodiak, and the wolf shifter ready to exchange. Once they're in the van and driving away, then Jo will walk Abbey in. No funny stuff, or else you'll never see your daughter. Deal?"

"It seems too easy," Edmund said. "I know you have something up your sleeve."

"Are you afraid?" Dad asked.

"Not in the least. But if Jo walks in, she's not walking out," Edmund said evenly.

"Jo can handle herself," Dad said then clicked off.

I puffed out my chest as an extra boost of adrenaline spiked in me. I needed all the encouragement I could get.

Olivia readied a crossbow. I'd only seen that weapon one time many months ago when one of the SEALs had been ready to use a crossbow on Jonah. The arrowheads were cobalt, and if inflicted directly into the heart, they would kill a vampire.

"Dad, any word on where Jonah is?" I asked.

Dad shifted the van into gear. "Jonah is not a concern."

"He should be," Webb said. "You trusted him, almost bringing him onto our team."

"We should be worried," Olivia chimed in. "Jonah has always been loyal to Edmund."

A muscle twitched in Webb's jaw. "And what about Dyson? Do we know if he's here?"

"According to Hollings, he's got a location on Dyson," Dad said. "He should be arresting him as we speak. Focus on what's about to happen. Jo, we'll be positioned far enough away but close enough to take out any of Edmund's men if we have to. Get out of the van but leave it running. Once Kraft, Kodiak, and Crysta are in the van, then walk in and not a minute sooner."

Webb placed his hand on the back of my neck. "Remember, we'll be inside within twenty-four hours at the most."

My heart began to race as fast as the cars that were speeding by, going in the opposite direction. "Abbey and I will be fine."

Within no time, Dad was pulling into an open and deserted parking lot. With the exception of Abbey, everyone got out. A hard wind blew, sending an icy chill through my body as I rounded the van to the driver's side.

Webb, Olivia, and Dad were clad in all black from their knitted hats right down to their boots. Daggers were strapped to their legs, swords at their waists, grenades hooked to their belts, and ear communicators tuned and ready to go.

Webb wrapped his strong arms around me. My stomach knotted as I melted into him. This could be the last time I see him or feel him again. "If I don't come back, will you promise me one thing?"

His gloved hand gently held my face. "Don't talk like that."

"Please. Just promise me you'll take care of Sam and my dad," I said, holding back all my emotions. "And please try and fall in love again."

He mashed his lips to mine, hard, fast, and with such vigor that I almost collapsed, and not from the strength behind his kiss but for the mere fact that this could be our last.

"Time to go," Dad said.

I heard Dad. I was sure Webb had as well. But it didn't stop us from memorizing each other.

A hand landed on my shoulder. "Jo, the sooner we get the show started, the sooner you can come back," Olivia said.

Webb let go first, and suddenly, ice coated my veins. We locked eyes until Dad stepped in between us.

"Pumpkin, you will return." He guided my chin up. "You're strong and powerful. Use your powers."

"I will if the warehouse isn't full of cobalt." The last time Edmund had kidnapped me, the rooms were made of cobalt, rendering my powers useless. It didn't matter, anyway. My powers would only stop a vampire long enough to get away, and the mission wasn't about fleeing. It was about killing.

"The mind-blocking potion should keep Edmund out of your head," Webb said. "It shouldn't wear off for a month."

I laughed nervously. "I hope I'm not in there for that long."

"Twenty-fours at most," Olivia delivered with confidence, and I believed her.

I got in the van before I decided to snag Webb and run as far away as we could. That cabin we'd stayed at in the Alaskan mountains sounded fantastic at the moment.

"Give us two minutes then head down. The warehouse will be one mile on the right," Dad said then closed my door.

I waited as they jogged down the road then out of sight.

"Jo," Abbey said. "My daddy won't hurt us."

I shifted into gear then glanced in the rearview mirror. Abbey had a smile on her face. "How do you know that?"

"I just do," she said.

I swore she acted older than five years old.

The warehouse came into view on my right. High fences bordered three sides of the perimeter, and like Crysta had mentioned, the fourth side of the warehouse disappeared into a mountainside. I stopped the van within thirty feet of the guard shack at the gate. The vast parking lot was desolate with the exception of one large eighteen-wheeler that was butted up to a roll-up door. Men patrolled the outer perimeter of the fence, while four were on top of the flat roof of the warehouse with guns at the ready.

I shifted into park, letting the engine idle, then climbed out, leaving the door open in the event I had to jump in and take off. As I opened the back door, I spotted the guard at the gate with a phone to his ear.

Abbey pointed out the windshield. "Look, Jo."

My pulse idled along with the engine, ready to sprint at any signs of trouble.

Two burly men shoved Kraft and Kodiak. Both stumbled but righted themselves. I didn't see Crysta. I glanced past Kraft and Kodiak, but saw nothing.

"I'll be right back," I said to Abbey. I inched closer to the SWAT-dressed vampire at the gate. "The deal was the wolf shifter too. Either get her out here or tell your boss the deal is off." I probably should've waited until Kraft and Kodiak were outside the fortress before I gave any ultimatums.

The guard snarled, showing me his fangs.

I lifted my right arm and squeezed the air with my hand. The gate guard grabbed his neck.

I held out my arm, squeezing the air harder, cutting off his ability to fill his lungs with oxygen. "If you want to breathe, make the call." I dropped my arm.

The guard choked as he tapped the screen of his phone. "The wolf shifter." His voice cracked.

When Kraft and Kodiak reached the gate, they nodded at me. Both vampires had blood-crusted hair, ripped uniforms, and beards that had grown in since they'd been abducted. Their appearance brought back memories of when Sam and I had found them deep in the Alaskan mountains after they'd been held for months as prisoners of Bruno Almeida.

Kraft, massive in size all the way around, narrowed his mahogany eyes at the gate guard. "I guess she put a hurt on you."

The red-faced vampire sneered at Kraft.

Kodiak snickered.

I opened a telepathic connection to both. *The deal includes Crysta. Have you seen her?*

Both shook their heads, while Kraft's nostrils flared. He and Crysta had some type of relationship. In my book, it was a love-hate relationship.

"Jo," Abbey called from behind us.

I peered down to find Abbey at my side. "We're not ready yet."

She pointed a finger toward the warehouse. "She's over there."

I followed her line of sight. Crysta jogged out, her long red hair whipping around in the wind. The burly guards in charge of Kraft and Kodiak stiffened.

The gate opened as Crysta sidled up to Kraft. Several cuts marred her face as though someone had taken the tip of a blade and scored her pretty skin.

Kraft swore. "I'll kill the man who did that to you."

Crysta tapped him on the chest. "Not now, vampire."

"Get in the van and go," I said to the three of them. "I'm not going in until you guys are on the road. Oh, and there's a note in the console on where to meet my dad. Hurry." I wanted to get the show started.

While Kraft and Kodiak hurried to the van, Crysta touched my arm. "The only way to get around inside is with someone's eyes."

I pinched my eyebrows together, but I didn't get a chance to ask her what she meant before Edmund's voice peppered the air.

Edmund rushed up, dressed in jeans, boots, and a turtleneck sweater that enhanced his sharp features. "Jo." The vampire's tone was almost giddy as though he hadn't seen me in quite some time.

"Go," I said to Crysta.

She hurried to the van, where Kraft was waiting behind the wheel. Kodiak sat in the back with his arm hanging out the door, ready to pull Crysta inside.

When the van's engine began to fade, I ambled in through the gate with Abbey's hand in mine.

Edmund squatted down as he scanned Abbey from head to toe. She wore a winter coat, scarf, and a furry pink hat, while her black hair hung freely.

As I witnessed a loving expression on Edmund's face, I realized how much Abbey and Edmund looked alike. They had the same straight nose, thick lips, and thick eyebrows. The only difference was the color of their eyes. Abbey had big blue eyes, and Edmund's were a muted brown color, almost yellow, depending on the light.

"Hi," Edmund said in a sugary tone. "I'm Edmund."

Abbey's cotton-candy-colored cheeks puffed out. "I'm Abbey."

"Well, Abbey, would you like to go inside?" Edmund asked. "I have your room ready with dolls and toys that you can play with."

"Only if Jo can come with me," Abbey said.

I narrowed my eyes at Edmund. "Where she goes, I go."

Edmund popped to his feet. "I'm glad you're here, Jo. I want you to help me train my new soldiers. Remember, we discussed you doing that very thing."

I swayed on my feet for a split second at the sincerity in his tone. Actually, I was suddenly speechless until a voice in the back of my mind told me to snap out of it. *He's still an enemy and a demon.*

We walked toward the warehouse in silence, Abbey holding on to me tightly. Edmund kept glancing at Abbey every now and then. Maybe with Edmund's fatherly and loving state of mind, I could talk some sense into him. *You're here to kill him, not get him on your side.*

My subconscious was spot-on. But first, I had to dance with the devil before I sent him to hell.

18

WEBB

I walked into a ballroom in the motel where we were staying, which was five miles north of Edmund's complex. For me, the distance was too far, but the motel had been the only one that would accommodate our request to rent out the entire property. We wanted complete privacy as we planned our next move. We couldn't take any chances on having Edmund's men snoop around or pretend they were guests in the hotel. Steven had even casually read the minds of five workers to be certain none of them knew of Edmund or worked at his warehouse.

Sam stalked in with bags of what smelled like hamburgers and tons of grease. My stomach rolled once at the idea of eating grease. As vampires, we needed protein, but my hunger was non-existent. Kraft followed Sam as though he was a starving vampire.

Kodiak trickled in too, sniffing the air. "I'm starving."

After Kodiak, Kraft, and Crysta had picked us up, we drove straight back to the motel. I wanted to grab a sleeping bag and head back out to keep an eye on the warehouse, which I would do once we knew what our next steps were.

Sam placed bags on each of the white-linen-covered tables on both sides of the aisle. Kodiak and Kraft plopped into chairs in the last row and began eating.

Steven and Olivia had grilled them on the way to the motel, but sadly, Kraft and Kodiak hadn't seen much. Crysta, on the other hand, had. We'd learned all the doors had top-of-the-line security with retina scans. Most of the large complex was empty, save for a section where supplies were offloaded. None of what we'd learned shocked me or gave me any reason to lose sight of our mission. Any one of those doors could be opened with a little C-4.

Sam dove into a bag and began eating his burger. In between bites, he said, "Webb eat. You'll need all the fuel you can get."

The only fuel I needed was adrenaline, and I had plenty to go around. In fact, I wouldn't relax until Jo was back in my arms. Hell, it had taken every ounce of willpower not to pull the trigger on the crossbow Olivia had given me and take out Edmund as he'd swaggered up to Jo and Abbey. The asshole had almost seemed human as he'd squatted down to talk to his daughter. But the minute they'd started for the building was the minute my heart sank to my feet and a deep coldness set in. I knew Jo could take care of herself, but the odds of her living through another dagger to the chest weren't high, at least not in my book. We had to get inside as fast as we could.

The rest of the team started to spill in, snatching burgers and fries as they found a seat at one of the classroom-style tables.

I poured a cup of coffee as Steven sidled up to me and did the same.

"Sawyer is working on hacking into the warehouse security system and their computers," Steven said. "If he can do that, then we won't need to carve out anyone's eyes to get in. I would like to get into that warehouse in the early morning hours when everyone is asleep. Otherwise, we'll have to wait until tomorrow night, and that is too damn long."

Boy, did I agree.

With his coffee in hand, Steven sauntered up to the PowerPoint projector that sat on a small table at the top of the aisle. "While everyone is eating, we're going to get started."

I hung back, standing near the last of the tables, where Kraft and Kodiak were sitting. Victor, Howell, Olivia, Tripp, Ben, Matthew, Sam, Crysta, and Dr. Vieira filled in the chairs ahead of me. The only person missing was Alia. She'd only tagged along to take care of Abbey.

The movie screen lit up, showing the blueprints of the building. "Crysta," Steven said. "Since you have the most knowledge, please come up and take us through these plans."

She followed orders, taking a laser pointer that had been on the table and pointing it at the screen. "I only can speak to what I saw, but before I was captured, I spoke to a couple of the locals about this building."

I still hadn't asked how she'd ended up in Edmund's custody. "Crysta, explain how they captured you," I said. Knowing how would keep us from walking into the same trap.

She nodded her red head. "A guard spotted me in my car with binoculars. I drove off before he had a chance to question me, but I was followed. As soon as I got out of my car at a bar in town, I was shot with a sedative. But the sedative didn't work that long. I might have been out for, at most, five minutes. When I woke up, we were driving through the gate of the warehouse. I did act like I was groggy in the event they decided to blindfold me."

"So," Dr. Vieira piped up. "Only five minutes?"

"Yeah, I suspect it's my wolf blood. Not a lot of drugs work on me unless I drink my cousin, Tripp's, vampire blood." She grinned at Tripp, who was sitting in the front row.

"Mmm," Dr. Vieira said. "I'll give you a shot of the antidote anyway before we leave."

Crysta pointed the laser at the screen. "They threw me in a room adjacent to these doors right here, which lead into the mountain. I only know that from listening to the people outside my door. The entire warehouse I think is a decoy in the event the law shows up. If they did, all they would see would be empty rooms and shelves with toilet paper, paper towels, drinks, etcetera. The bottom line is nothing in the warehouse says there's a medical lab, an army of humans turned vampire, or anything of the like. Edmund's operation is in the mountain. Probably deep in the mountain."

"So blowing up the building wouldn't get us far?" Victor asked. He was sitting next to Tripp.

"Kodiak and I were in a sterile room with thick cobalt doors," Kraft said. "When they escorted us out, we passed through a large empty room with high ceilings. That was it."

Steven folded his arms over his chest. "But the outside doors we can see are governed by retina scans?"

Crysta nodded. "That was how the guy who captured me got inside."

"How are we going to get my sister and Abbey out?" Sam asked from where he sat in the back row, opposite Kraft and Kodiak.

I cleared my throat. "First, Edmund knows we're here. He knows that we're going to do everything possible to get Jo out. Second, he's a former SEAL. So he's learned not to barricade himself in. That tells me two things. One, he's probably getting ready to take Abbey and Jo away from here, which leads me to the second. He has another entry point in and out through the mountain."

The room dropped into a dead silence.

Tripp rose, gathering his trash. "Then Webb and I will go hiking. Because no blueprint is going to show us a mountain access."

I had to love my best friend. He was a take-no-prisoners kind of vampire.

Steven dipped his head once at me. "Victor, Sam, Olivia, and Ben, take two vehicles and head out toward the complex. The four of you replace four of the vampire guards and patrol the area. I don't want to call attention to their security just yet. Leave the human guards intact. In the meantime, Kraft and Kodiak, Viking II will be rolling in within the hour. I want you both to bring them up to speed then take them a mile outside the warehouse and do some surveillance. Matthew, I want you to help Dr. Vieira. He'll be administering the antidote to Viking II."

Howell raised his hand. "Commander, what would you like me to do?"

"You're with me," Steven said. "You know the area. Let's head into town and snoop around. If anything goes down, then alert the team."

Ben stalked up, all six feet of him. "I'm ready," he said as he regarded me.

I slapped him on the arm. "I know you are. Listen to Olivia."

Steven joined us as his phone rang. "I've got to take this in private. Tripp and Webb, if you find anything in the mountains, call in." He ambled out of the room.

With the orders doled out, everyone scattered, including Tripp and me.

Within five minutes, Tripp and I were on the road. He drove while I navigated.

"If we find any access, we're going in." I wasn't waiting. The longer we sat, the more of a chance Edmund had to flee.

Tripp turned down a dirt road. "If we do, we call the commander, then we go in."

I scratched my neck. "Good. Because when we call the commander, he'll tell us to wait for his orders."

Tripp pulled off and parked the SUV in an opening between two large tree trunks. "Every time we do things by the book when it comes to Edmund, we walk away empty-handed or someone gets killed. That isn't happening tonight. Tonight, we go rogue if we have to."

I was his leader. I should be correcting him. But I didn't see any other way to get Jo and Abbey out alive, kill Edmund, and destroy Patrick's research.

We gathered our gear and weapons then headed out into the night.

19

JO

Abbey was asleep in my arms as Edmund gave me a tour of the facility. An odd sense of weirdness settled in my stomach as my number one enemy pointed out different areas of his fortress as though he was leading a group of tourists through a museum. Nothing he showed me was fascinating. I'd seen walls made of rock, felt cold air, smelled dirt and must, and sadly, I'd seen glass rooms that had humans strapped to tables. As we traversed the part of the complex that was embedded in the mountain, that weirdness in my stomach morphed into nausea. Innocent humans were about to be or had been experimented on. Not only that, memories of when I'd found my brother, Sam, in a glass room on his deathbed shot the nausea in my stomach off the charts.

I ground my teeth, tempering my anger and willing the bile creeping up into my throat to go away as we stopped at a thick steel door.

"Why don't I hold her?" Edmund asked. "It appears you need a break."

I mentally scratched my head at his kind voice, his warm expression, and how proud he was of his operation. The latter didn't surprise me. After all, Edmund had boasted about how he would build an army. And I shouldn't have been that shocked that he was being nice. He'd been kind to me at the lab on the Indian reservation. But at the moment, his warm-hearted demeanor was overly excessive. I was also shocked that he wasn't nervous about my dad and his team lurking outside his complex. Maybe Abbey's presence was triggering a side of Edmund no one had seen.

Edmund waved a hand in front of me. "Jo?"

"Why are you so nice?" I asked. "You know my father is going to try and get me out of this place."

He took Abbey into his arms. She stirred for a second before snuggling her head into the crook of his neck.

He briefly closed his eyes as though Abbey was the drug he needed. "First, my daughter needs to see the real me. And as far as your father, there's no way in. I know how he thinks, so I'm prepared. He can force my guards on the outside for information. He won't get it. He can blow up doors. He still won't get in."

I guessed I shouldn't have been too surprised at how prepared he was for my dad's onslaught. But I was definitely thrown off track by his thick sweetness. "You've been an evil man since I met you. Abbey will see through that."

He rubbed Abbey's back. "We all have an evil side, Jo, even your father and Webb."

"They act in self-defense or to protect innocent humans and vampires," I countered.

Edmund positioned his eyes into a scanner adjacent to the steel door. "And how is that any different? Killing someone is all the same."

With a whoosh, the door slid open. Stark white lights spilled out as a gust of sterile air washed over me.

"After you," Edmund said.

I hesitated as I searched the inside of the room. In no way was I getting locked up. But the lab benches, beakers, a large oven, and my uncle Patrick standing over a microscope didn't portray a prison cell. Then again, the setup did give me the willies, especially with Abbey present. Dad had suspected that Edmund would use his daughter as a lab rat, and I couldn't let that happen.

"I'm not taking your DNA or Abbey's," Edmund said, as though he could read my thoughts. But I knew he couldn't since I'd taken the mind-blocking potion. "I told you when we walked in earlier that I would show you around. And your uncle wanted to see you and meet my daughter."

A hysterical laugh broke out in my head. The only reason my uncle wanted to see me would be to take a sample of my DNA or Abbey's. "Then give me Abbey."

Edmund cocked a dark eyebrow. "I give you my word."

"And that's supposed to mean something?" I asked.

My uncle Patrick wiped his hands on his lab coat as he crossed the cement floor. "Jo, it's so good to see you." He raked his sky-blue gaze over me. "How's my brother?" His tone was disgustingly sweet.

I had to be in an alternate universe or dreaming. "My dad wants you dead." I didn't see a reason to lie.

A condescending laugh rumbled out of Patrick before he banked his attitude. "So this is Abbey?"

Edmund's lips tipped upward as he clung to his daughter.

"Why did you kill her mother?" I asked Edmund.

He ushered me inside, and I went willingly, although I stayed close to the door.

Abbey stirred then blinked several times before she pushed away from Edmund. "I want Jo."

Edmund didn't protest as he handed her to me, seemingly not the least bit hurt from what I could tell.

Immediately, Abbey locked her arms around my neck as she set her sleepy blue eyes on my uncle Patrick. "You'll die soon," she said so seriously.

Bewildered expressions swept over Patrick and Edmund's faces. I was sure I had one of those looks too. I knew Abbey had visions, but to hear her say those words with such conviction sent a chill down my spine—a chill coated with equal parts sadness and excitement. After all, Patrick was kin, but he was a bad seed in our family lineage—a jealous boy who had grown up to hate my father because my dad was a vampire and he wasn't. Needless to say that in order to keep our existence as vampires out of the hands and knowledge of the human government, Patrick needed to disappear, die, or have his memories wiped. At the very least, we had to erase his memories and destroy all physical data.

Patrick shoved his hands into his lab coat. "How do you know this, Abbey?"

"I see into the future," she said with the cutest smile.

I resisted the urge to kiss her cotton-candy-colored cheeks or jump up and down for joy at how she'd rendered them speechless. I didn't want to do anything that would upset Edmund to the point that he would take Abbey away from me.

Slow and sharp, Edmund's fangs elongated. "Not possible."

Abbey buried her face in my neck.

"Put the fangs away. You're scaring her." I walked deeper into the lab, holding on to Abbey as though her life depended on it. I should've been walking out the door. But one, I didn't have a way out or know where to go. And two, my throat was parched to the point that if I didn't get blood, I would collapse. I opened the small refrigerator that sat on a counter along the right wall, hoping they kept a blood supply.

Small bottles of blood lined the top shelf. I grabbed one then turned back to face the gaping duo, who were staring at Abbey and me. *Wow.* If a vision of Patrick's future was all it took to stop them dead in their tracks, then Abbey needed to tell them more about how neither of them would live to see tomorrow.

I examined the label on the bottle. All signs said the contents had come from a blood bank in Anchorage, so I didn't have to worry about drinking poisoned or drug-laced blood.

"Edmund, she is your daughter. Why are you so surprised?"

He shook his head once, his eyes flickering from brown to

vampire red. "Supernatural powers are passed down from someone in a vampire's lineage. There is no one in my family who has been able to see into the future. The only one I've ever known to have that power is your grandfather, Jo."

I set Abbey down on the top of the lab bench in the middle of the room. For a split second, I thought about Edmund's statement. If that were true, then Edmund was related to me. Dad hadn't said anything about another brother. Patrick was Dad's half brother, and while it was possible that Edmund could have been related to the Mason family, I didn't believe it for a second. Or maybe he was trying to say that Abbey was not his daughter but rather my dad's child. Still, I had to ask. "So what are you saying?"

"Abbey could be your father's daughter," Edmund said.

"Nope. I know for a fact you're her father. Dr. Vieira tested Abbey's DNA against yours. Apparently, he had your data from when you were part of the SEAL team. Trust me. I wanted to know if you could be her father." I remembered asking Dad that very question. "Not only that, look at her. She has your nose, hair, and lips. So someone in your long history of vampires had to have strong supernatural powers. I mean, why do your eyes change to red? With the exception of my dad and me, all vampire eyes are black."

Patrick went over to the sink. "It's part of his DNA. It was a question I had as well. And Edmund isn't related to the Mason family. I also tested his DNA against mine and your father's."

"There you have it," I added with a sigh. Regardless, if he had been related to us, it wouldn't have changed our mission. He would still have to die.

Edmund waltzed up to Abbey, studying her features. "She does have my nose. And I don't know my family lineage well."

Once Edmund's fangs were no longer in view, Abbey reached out and flattened her palm on his unshaven jaw.

I held my breath. Anytime Abbey touched a person's face, she showed them a vision.

Patrick gulped down a glass of water. The sound echoed around the room as he and I watched Edmund's expression flicker from confusion to happiness to shock. When Abbey dropped her hand, Edmund's face paled to a blinding shade of white.

Edmund gripped the back of his neck. "Impossible."

Lines dented Patrick's forehead. "What did you see?"

Edmund plucked his phone from his jeans pocket. "Blow up the warehouse so no one gets in. Do it now!"

My pulse picked up speed for many reasons, but one stuck out. "What did Abbey show you?" The blood I was drinking curdled in my stomach.

Patrick opened a drawer near the sink, produced a handgun, and proceeded to point it at Abbey.

Holy shit! I dropped the bottle, blood splattering everywhere as I grabbed Abbey.

Edmund threw himself in between Patrick and me. "Put the gun down, Patrick."

I leaned out to see around Edmund's big body.

Patrick pinched his eyebrows together so hard, his eyes were barely open. "The girl says I'm going to die. Like hell I am."

I searched behind me for a weapon but found nothing. I could have used my elemental magic, but then I might risk hurting Abbey.

"She's too young to know anything." Edmund's tone wasn't convincing. Then he lifted his phone to his ear. "Get to the lab."

"Edmund, what did Abbey show you?" I asked at his back.

He whirled around. "It appears that my daughter has quite the visions. She showed me how you're going to kill me." His expression was blank, but his tone made the hairs on the back of my neck stand up.

Suddenly, I regretted bringing Abbey in with me. Now Edmund knew how I would kill him. The funny part was I didn't even know how I would kill him.

Abbey trembled against me. The last time I'd seen her scared was when Webb and I found her in the electrical room beneath the scoring booth of the baseball field on base. She'd been hiding from a man in the woods who had red eyes, but it had turned out to be Ben and not Edmund.

"It's okay," I said in her ear. "He's not going to hurt you."

"I know, but he's going to take you away from me," she cried.

"Shh." I had to figure something out. But first I needed to know how I was supposed to kill Edmund. "Abbey, can you tell me how I'm going to kill Edmund?"

Edmund plucked Abbey out of my arms and covered her mouth with his big hand. "She will not."

Before I could do anything, Jonah's big body graced the doorway. "Sir?"

I snarled. The vampire who my dad had believed and trusted to defect from enemy territory was back and working for his old boss. So many memories accosted me about Jonah. He had always been there to do Edmund's dirty work.

"Take Jo to a cell," Edmund ordered, holding Abbey tightly.

She scratched his face. When he released his hand from her mouth, she bit his nose. Edmund pulled her off him, and as soon as he did, Abbey jumped out of his arms and flew out the door, faster than the speed of light.

Once my brain rebooted from the comical scene, I ran too. "Abbey!"

I made it a foot outside the lab when Edmund shoved me against the wall. "Jonah, do as I ordered."

Jonah's large paw landed on my arm. "Not so fast."

Edmund sprinted down the long, desolate hall.

Abbey's little body faded from view the farther down the hall she ran. When she got to the end, she waved a hand, and a door opened.

Jonah dragged me back into the lab. "Patrick, hand me the gun."

I laughed. "That gun won't kill me." I checked up and down the hall. Edmund and Abbey were nowhere in sight. I swept my hand from right to left, much like Abbey had done. But the lab door didn't move. I tried again as Patrick tossed the gun to Jonah.

"I told you that won't kill me," I said. "You know that."

He aimed the gun at me.

Again, I wanted to laugh out loud at how bizarrely things were unfolding. Granted, the bullets would slow me down, but Jonah knew better. I balled my fists at my sides, conjuring up anger, which always kick-started my telekinesis. I at least needed a distraction to get out of there. I had a five-year-old to find before Edmund did something stupid to his child.

A shot rang out, piercing my eardrums.

I froze, mentally scanning my body for a bullet. Not a lick of pain coursed through me. I blinked once, then Jonah fired off another shot. This time, the bullet whizzed by my ear. I whirled around to find Patrick falling to the floor.

My jaw hit my feet, bounced back, then slammed into the tips of my boots again. I swallowed hard and fast, gulping down as much saliva as I could. "I don't understand."

I listened for Patrick's heartbeat, and as Jonah crossed the lab, Patrick's heart stopped.

"I told your father I was on his side, and I never go back on my word." Jonah bent over Patrick's dead body. Blood was quickly soaking my uncle's white lab coat. Jonah dipped into the inside of Patrick's lab coat and produced a key.

I shook the cobwebs loose. "What is that for? And please explain what the hell is going on." I wanted to trust Jonah, but what if he had orders from Edmund to kill Patrick? Maybe I'd missed that signal when Edmund summoned Jonah.

"This key is to an office complex where Patrick keeps all his research data. The walls are about to shake like an extremely bad earthquake. So we need to bolt."

"I'm not going with you." I ran out of the lab then stopped. I needed him if I were going to get through doors.

He came up beside me. "You realized you need me? I know that you're skeptical, but I promise I'm here to shut Edmund down. Don't you think killing Patrick is proof enough?"

He had a point. "Give me the key." I held out my hand.

He considered me for a long moment, his nostrils opening wide. "If you want to save Abbey, then we should get going."

"I said to give me the key."

He loomed over me, showing long canines. "The only person that gets this key is your father."

I bared my own fangs, deciding my next move. His tone seemed genuine, which didn't match his predatory look. Regardless, I needed him. "Fine. But if my dad doesn't get that key, then you're a dead man."

He retracted his fangs then ran down the hall. As I put one foot in front of the other, the walls shook and the lights flickered.

"Come on, Jo," Jonah yelled.

I rushed down the hall as another boom rocked the mountain. Dust from the ceiling rained down. When I reached Jonah, he had his eyes positioned over the security scanner adjacent to the steel door.

With a whoosh, the door slid open. Then we were traveling down another long, deserted hall. The air became colder the further we ran.

"Where does this lead to?" I asked.

"To an emergency exit."

I stopped short. "I can't leave without Abbey."

Jonah kept going. "The door Abbey went through only leads one way and that's to Edmund's emergency exit."

Great. If they got out of the building, then we would lose them for sure. In vampire speed, I caught up to Jonah. We turned down another hall then another until we couldn't go any farther.

"I'll warn you," Jonah said. "Beyond this steel door is a room full of engineered vampires. Monsters if you ask me."

I didn't care about makeshift vampires, but Abbey was human, and in a room full of humans turning vampire, that wouldn't be good with their blood thirst.

Before he could open the door, another explosion rocked the halls, then the lights went out.

The blood drained from my face. "Um… Jonah? Please tell me you can get through that steel door."

Within seconds, my vampire vision kicked in. Jonah now appeared grayish in my line of sight.

He was tapping numbers on the keypad. "We're screwed."

"No way. We have to beat down that door."

He sucked in air. "All our vampire strength won't break down that door."

Which was why Edmund had said my father wouldn't be able to get in.

My stomach tossed and turned with nausea. "What is the backup plan when the lights go out?"

"There is none. The keypads and scanners don't work unless we have power."

I started to run back the way we came until I saw that the walls had caved in. Regardless, I jogged up as far as I could to see if there was any way we could crawl through. Just as I reached the rubble, the lights flickered on.

"Jo," Jonah called. "Let's go before they go out again."

As I returned, the hall went dark. Not being able to do anything was maddening. "Keep your eyes over the scanner so when the lights come on again, the door will open." At least I hoped the lights would come on and the door would open.

Jonah didn't move. I dared not go back and try to find a way out, at least not for the next few minutes. As I waited, I could barely hear moans and cries for help on the other side of the door.

I took in a deep breath of dusty air when, for a split second, the hall brightened. Jonah's eyes widened, and the door opened at most a foot before the power died again.

"I can get through." I wasn't sure about Jonah, but he wasn't fat so he would hopefully be able to squeeze his broad body through the opening.

As soon as I stepped through, a powerful stench of death and human fear made me choke. "Wow!" I pinched my nose, worried I might pass out just from the rancid odor.

The room was pitch-black, but I could see with no problem. Faint cries of help made their way to my ears.

Jonah came through the opening. "Holy hell." He fiddled in his pocket, pulled out a cell phone, and turned on the flashlight.

I gasped when my gaze landed on piles of dead bodies scattered around the cavernous room.

"This whole serum and experiment just isn't working," Jonah said. "It's really sad."

We didn't have time to mourn. "Abbey couldn't have come this way." From where I stood, we were trapped once again.

"She did. As you saw on our way here, no other exits existed," Jonah said. "And I heard that Edmund had a way out of the mountain through this room." He slowly waved his phone around.

Each time the light landed on a dead body or a barely moving body, pain gripped my chest. The humans didn't deserve to die.

"Stay close," Jonah said.

He and I slowly walked around the room, stepping over body after body until a hand grabbed my ankle. I flinched and squealed before I looked down.

A petite dark-haired girl, whose eyes were protruding way too far out of their sockets, moved her mouth.

I bent down.

"Jo, you can't help her," Jonah said.

"Please get me out of here," the girl whispered.

My heart broke in half as the anger I harbored for Edmund made me growl loudly. I peeled the girl's hand off me. As much as I wanted to help her, Jonah was right. Her pulse was slowing, and at any second, she would take her last breath.

Jonah nudged me. "Up there."

I rose and followed Jonah's line of sight. A small doorway was carved into the mountain high above us. I searched for a way up. All I found was a ladder bolted to the wall, similar to the fire escape ladders on buildings. But from my angle, Abbey wouldn't have been able to reach that.

"Impossible that Abbey could get up there," I said.

"She could if Edmund carried her."

I started for the ladder. Maybe it was movable like those on a fire escape. I didn't get far, when a bright flash followed by an explosion rocked the earth beneath my feet, sending me flying through the air. My back hit rock. Pain shot through my chest as the wind left my lungs. I fell face-first on top of a dead body. I pushed to my feet only to fall again. Nausea threatened as I tried to orient my vision.

"Jo," Jonah called. "You've got a vampire coming your way."

I wiped the dust from my face and again rose on shaky legs. A blurry figure moved toward me. The closer he got, the bigger he got.

Grunts ensued off to my left as bones cracked.

Suddenly, a light was shining in my direction. I peeled my gaze away from the unfamiliar beefy vampire and found Jonah stalking toward me.

"Behind you," I shouted at Jonah.

Jonah spun around and landed a roundhouse kick to his attacker's face. Grunts sounded once again.

The beefy vampire headed toward me seemed to have problems navigating the dead bodies on the floor. So I took the fight to him. I marched over bodies, my fangs extended, my fists ready to do damage. But I didn't have a chance against the dagger in his hand. The only recourse I had was my elemental magic. It wouldn't kill the vampire, but it would slow him down.

I found the floor in between two bodies and stomped my foot hard. The room shook as a jolt of the earth's power engulfed me. Then, quick as lightning, I lifted both arms, closed my fingers together as though I was gripping someone's neck, and clamped down on the air. The vampire grasped his throat, the dagger falling from his hand. His black eyes protruded before he collapsed. I turned around and repeated the process on the seven-foot-tall vampire fighting with Jonah.

When he fell to the ground, someone began clapping. "Quite a talent, Jo," Edmund said from above.

"Jo," Abbey cried.

I blinked several times, swinging my gaze upward. When I did, my heart stopped. Edmund was dangling Abbey in the air.

"She's your daughter, for God's sake," I cried.

"She's a means to an end," Edmund said.

All I could think about was what my grandfather had said about Abbey dying.

I leapt over bodies until I was under Abbey. "Abbey, I want you to be brave." I eyed the ladder, but I knew that the minute I got to the ladder was the minute Edmund would let her go.

It didn't matter how far up Abbey was. Any fall could kill a human if the person landed the right way.

Jonah darted over to the ladder.

"That ladder won't work," Edmund said. "I locked it in place."

I couldn't use my elemental magic. If I sucked the air from Edmund's lungs, it would only cause him to drop her. Maybe that wouldn't be a bad thing. Jonah and I could catch her.

"Jo," Abbey said. "I'm not afraid. Webb is coming."

Edmund let out a roar of laughter. "He won't get past my guards."

"Edmund," Jonah said. "It's all over. Your operation is a bust. I mean, look at all the dead bodies down here that didn't make it. That serum will never work, even if you start again. You can't keep killing innocent humans."

"Traitor," Edmund said in a disgusted tone. "Why, Jonah?"

Jonah growled. "Because you killed the only girl I ever loved. You weren't supposed to use her."

Edmund's eyes glowed red. "When you were captured by Mason, she begged me to turn her."

All of sudden, Webb was in my head. *Catch Abbey.*

I pulled Jonah closer to me. "Open your arms."

In a blur, a man in black tackled Edmund, propelling them through the air. I focused on Abbey as did Jonah. I was strong enough to catch her, but I wasn't sure if I had the stamina to stay upright. As she fell, I held my breath until Jonah moved me just an inch and Abbey fell into his arms.

I grabbed Abbey and hugged her to me. "I'm so glad you're okay."

"You need to kill Edmund," she said. "Hurry. There's not much time."

Jonah's eyebrows went up into his hairline.

I handed Abbey back to Jonah. I didn't know how I was supposed to kill Edmund, but when I turned, my vision almost blurred. I watched in horror as Edmund stuck a dagger into Webb's chest. Webb stumbled over bodies. Just as he was about to fall, Edmund grabbed Webb's sword from his waist.

I screamed as Webb's blood scented the air. It was all I could do not to let my rage blind me. I didn't care that Edmund stalked toward me with a three-foot sword pointed at me. I had to get to Webb.

I was so consumed with fury that I tripped over a body. As I righted myself, Edmund pointed the tip of the blade at my throat.

He gave me a wicked smile. "Now you can't kill me. I have the weapon that Abbey envisioned you using to kill me. So I'm not dying after all. And I will enjoy watching you die."

I froze, my mind searching furiously for a way to get the sword from him. Not only that, but one wrong move on my part, and the blade would be slicing through skin and bone. I tried to divert only my eyes to check on Webb, but I couldn't find him. My pulse beat rapidly, and I was ready to vomit.

"Webb," I called. "Please tell me you're alive."

Abbey started to cry. *Oh my God.* If she was crying, then something bad had happened to Webb. She must've seen a vision of his death.

"Webb," I called again. Out of the corner of my eye, I saw Jonah heading in Webb's direction with Abbey in his arms.

Edmund laughed as he plunged the sword into my throat. Visions of him stabbing Rachel and images of my past scrambled into focus. One incident in particular in which Cliff had stabbed me made me falter where I stood. Death seemed so close.

But I couldn't die with a sword to the throat. So despite the blood oozing out of my mouth and the fact that I couldn't swallow, I stomped my foot on the dirt-packed floor, allowing the earth's energy to consume me once again. Then I fisted my hands at my sides. The ground shook around Edmund and me. Then the floor cracked, and the earth moved, creating a chasm that separated Edmund and me from Jonah, Abbey, and Webb. I kept my fists closed as the earth continued to move, the chasm growing larger. Bodies of the poor humans rolled off into the dark abyss.

"Jonah," I called. His name came out garbled as though I was gargling mouthwash. Blood pooled in the back of my throat.

Edmund twisted the sword to the right.

I winced, trying to swallow, but that only served to increase the pain as blood began to dribble out of my mouth.

I narrowed my eyes at my enemy, shaking my head as an idea formed. I slowly walked forward. As I did, Edmund had no choice but to walk backward toward the large chasm.

"Jo, what are you doing?" Webb asked in a deep and fearful voice.

Tears poured out, hot and fast, at the sound of Webb's voice. The vampire gods were on my side, or maybe my grandfather was. *Grandfather, if you can hear me or are with me, please help me find a way to kill Edmund.*

Edmund wobbled on the edge of the cliff. If he fell, he could take me with him. Or he could let go of the sword. But neither scenario bothered me as much as the thought that if he fell, he wouldn't die. I stopped.

"Jo," Webb pleaded. "Please don't do this. I can't lose you."

Laughter bubbled out of Edmund's mouth. "Well, it doesn't seem like that's your choice, Webb."

"Webb." Abbey sniffled. "Jo needs that sword. Or else she will die."

I rushed to figure out a way I could get the sword from Edmund.

Edmund grinned. "If I fall, I won't die."

He may have been right, and I couldn't take that chance. So I stepped back, inch by inch, and as I did, I grasped the blade. If I could get the sword out of my throat, I might stand a chance of using it on Edmund.

Edmund swayed. Blood steadily oozed out of my mouth, the iron taste not as yummy as it usually was. I started counting in my head. *One. Two.* And on three, I yanked the sword out of my throat as quickly as I could. Edmund listed to one side, his grip loosening on the handle. The sword fell with a clang.

Edmund and I scrambled for the weapon. He knocked me out of the way, and I rolled to the edge, almost falling over into the chasm. Quickly, I popped to my feet and lunged at Edmund. He went down hard on his back with an *oof.*

I ripped the sword out of his hand.

He scrambled to his feet, examining his option to jump.

Not happening.

I gripped the sword with both hands and made one sweeping motion that I had practiced over and over in the training room. I spun around, and with all the power and muscle I could muster, I struck. The blade sliced through cartilage and bone.

Edmund's head flew off in the direction where Webb, Jonah, and Abbey were standing. I was relieved to see that Webb had Abbey's face tucked into him so she couldn't see anything.

Edmund's headless body stumbled and wobbled before falling into the canyon of the earth.

I collapsed to my knees, spitting up blood as all the adrenaline rushed out of me. I couldn't say for sure if I was freaked out about chopping off Edmund's head or elated that he was finally dead.

"Jo," Webb called.

"Jo," Abbey echoed.

I glanced over at them and sighed as tears spilled out.

Webb gave Abbey to Jonah, then he jumped. I held my breath. There had to be a good hundred feet separating us. I knew as vampires, we were agile, but I'd never tested my ability to jump that far.

He landed without any problem, and before I could say a word, he angled his neck. I didn't hesitate. My fangs went in deep as I sucked his blood into me. The first sip was like a soothing gel as it coated my throat, and all I could think about was that I was finally free.

20

WEBB

A bright light streamed from the flashlight Steven held in his hand as he jumped down from the high doorway, the same one I'd tackled Edmund from.

"Mander," Abbey squealed.

Jo retracted her fangs and licked her lips.

I gently rubbed the area on her neck where the blade had punctured her. It was almost closed. "You gave me a heart attack."

"The feeling is mutual." Her voice was hoarse.

I smoothed her hair back. "The dagger hit a lung. I couldn't breathe until Jonah gave me blood."

"And you didn't wear your protective vest," she said.

I didn't want to talk. I knew I shouldn't do what I was about to do with her father in the cavernous room. But I didn't care. I captured her lips in mine, pushing my tongue in her mouth. Tasting her blood, I took all I could to get my pulse to slow. Ever since she'd walked into Edmund's fortress, I'd been afraid I would never get the chance to kiss her again.

She eased back, breathing heavy as tears streamed down her face.

I wiped a tear away with my fingers. "What's wrong?"

"I'm happy we're alive. That's all."

I was beyond happy. We could get on with our lives, although we had some cleanup to do first. I helped Jo to her feet. "Let's go."

She stiffened. "I've never jumped that far before." She pointed to the other side of the chasm, where her father was studying Edmund's head.

Beyond Steven, Jonah was helping Abbey climb up the ladder to the opening, which was the only way out. I'd learned before I stormed in that Edmund had blown up the warehouse along with the access to get inside.

"All you have to do is concentrate," I said.

She let out a nervous laugh. Then she took a few steps back before she jumped and screamed at the same time. She landed near her dad, who caught her before she splattered forward.

I followed, smiling the whole time.

Steven threw his arms around Jo. "I'm so glad you're alive."

I sighed with Steven as I checked on Abbey. Sam was at the entrance, lifting her off the ladder. Once she was safe, Jonah climbed the rest of the way.

Jo let go of her dad, snagged his flashlight, and panned it around the room. "All these innocent people he killed just to experiment on. I guess I'll never understand why Ben and Matthew survived with the serum but not these people."

"We know why Matthew made it through," Steven said. "And Dr. Vieira will tell you that Ben's DNA shows some strong properties that align with a vampire's DNA."

"Since when?" Jo asked. "I didn't know that about Ben."

I didn't, either.

"Dr. Vieira has had his hands full," Steven said. "But we'll be able to use Ben's DNA data to explain to his father why Ben's eyes change to red."

Jo's voice rose. "Does that mean you're going to tell Mr. Jackson about vampires?"

Steven shook his head. "I believe it's in our best interest not to. Ben doesn't and won't have fangs. He won't have a thirst for blood. His added strength and eye color change can easily be explained with DNA data."

I grabbed Jo's hand. "I agree with your dad. We don't need more humans knowing about us. And Ben is learning to control his emotions."

She chewed on her lip as she looked around. "You're right. If Mr. Jackson did know about vampires, then he might want to become one. And I wouldn't wish that on him, not after seeing all these dead humans."

Sam came down. "Whoa!" He examined Edmund's head, focusing on the eyes, which were wide open. "You did this, huh, Sis?"

Jo threw her arms around her brother.

"I'm good, Sis."

"I know," she said. "I'm just happy to see you."

Steven clapped a hand on my back. "Webb, I owe you and Tripp for finding that damn entrance. How did you, by the way?"

"Heat signatures were strong around that area. It also helped that Edmund had an all-terrain vehicle waiting with a vampire in it when Tripp and I approached."

Steven picked up Edmund's head. "For so long, this guy was a dear and close friend to me. Everything he's done since leaving the military is my fault."

Jo's mouth opened slightly. "It is not."

Steven nodded. "If I hadn't pushed the council of elders to dishonorably discharge him instead of throwing him in prison for killing Ella Case, then we wouldn't have gone through hell and back. Jo and Sam, I'm so sorry for everything you both have been through."

"Pops," Sam said. "Jo and I haven't had an easy life with foster care then becoming vampires. But if I had to do it all over again, I wouldn't change the vampire part. What happened with Edmund brought you to us. And while I hated you in the beginning, I don't blame you for what has happened to us in the last year."

Steven met Sam, eye to eye. "But you still blame me for foster care?"

Sam gripped his father's shoulder. "That's all in the past. I'm your son, and I love and respect you."

Jo slipped her fingers in mine. "Dad, I agree with Sam. If the course of events from that day when my foster dad stabbed me didn't happen, then I wouldn't have met Webb." She peered up at me with love in her eyes then regarded her father. "And I wouldn't have met you. We're a family now. And Webb will be your son-in-law. So can we please go home? I have a wedding to plan."

After eyeing Edmund's head one more time, Steven walked over to the edge of the earth and tossed the head into the black abyss.

If that wasn't the ending to close up the past, then I didn't know what was.

All of us stood in silence for two heartbeats before Steven sighed heavily. "Let's go home."

Man, that sounded fantastic. The realization of the mission, Edmund's death, my future with Jo, starting a family, getting out of the military, getting married, and most of all, making love to Jo hit me like a F5 tornado. My stomach knotted, my pulse sped up, and all I wanted to do was sweep Jo into my arms and take her right there. But she deserved a plush suite, soft music, champagne, and a bed of rose petals rather than dirt, dead bodies, and a dungeon.

As we made our way out, Jo explained to us how Jonah had killed Patrick.

"So Steven, that phone call you got at the hotel before Tripp and I left, that was Jonah?"

Steven nodded as we exited through the door in the mountain. The crisp air was a welcome relief over the stench in the dungeon.

"I couldn't tell anyone," Steven said. "When I heard he and Dyson had fled, I got ahold of Jonah. I didn't know how successful

Jonah would be, but I had asked him to take out my brother first chance he had."

I trudged through the thicket. "And Dyson's motivation for siding with Edmund? Did Jonah explain that part?"

"Apparently, Dyson's reason was merely family," Steven said from behind me. "He has a sister who lost the chance to make the change from human to vampire because their father passed too soon. So he funded half of Edmund's operation."

I'd been way off base. I would've sworn Dyson wanted money or power. Regardless, I owed Jonah for giving me blood so I could heal so quickly and also for being there for Jo. I had seriously thought that when I finally got into the fortress, I would find Jo's dead body. Then again, that thought paled in comparison to the memory of my sword embedded in Jo's throat.

I shook off that image. Man, I had so many memories of near-death experiences that it would take an eternity to erase them all. But I didn't care. I had Jo to help me forget all the bad that had happened in my life.

21

JO

After four weeks of preparation, my big day was finally here. I stood in front of a mirror in an upstairs bedroom in Victor's mansion, staring at myself and willing the nervous nellies to quiet down inside me.

Since we'd gotten back from Alaska, life had been refreshing, crazy, joyous, and to some extent, a little strange. It had taken a week after our return for Edmund's death to sink in. Even then, the notion that I wouldn't be fighting, running, or always looking over my shoulder for Edmund hadn't come to light until I started planning my wedding. Dad hadn't protested when I wanted to go shopping. He hadn't sent bodyguards with me. I could hang out with Darcy without worrying if one of Edmund's men would turn up and kidnap one of us.

I sighed, thinking about how Webb would react when he saw me in my wedding dress. I'd hardly seen him in the last couple of weeks, and that was probably a good thing since we couldn't keep our hands off each other and he was still being a gentleman. My pulse sped up at the notion that tonight would be the night we would make love for the first time. Yeah, my heart was full-on galloping at that thought since I'd never had sex before. It wasn't that I was scared. I knew Webb would be gentle, but my fear was whether I would be good or know what to do. Out of all of our make-out sessions, I had kissing and groping down to a science, but nothing else.

I took in slow and even breaths as the door squeaked open. Darcy glided in with her blond hair twisted up in a fancy style, much like mine. Her red dress hugged her curves as the satin fabric pooled to her feet. I'd wanted red for my maid of honor and my bridesmaids, Olivia, Alia, and Crysta. The color was festive and matched the pretty poinsettias that were scattered around the mansion along with the Christmas decorations.

"The guests are arriving," Darcy said. "Are you ready?"

I inhaled then shivered. "I am. Maybe a little nervous."

She giggled. "You should be. It's your big day. And you look absolutely beautiful." She went over to the chair near the fireplace and grabbed my veil. "Turn around."

I faced the mirror once again while she secured the veil to the back of my hair, which was braided into a twist. I'd wanted a dress that was simple, and I'd found one almost immediately when I'd entered a dress shop in the city. The sheath gown had a beaded bodice, empire waist, and capped sleeves. It was made of satin and crepe with a sweep train that fell to the floor elegantly.

"There," she said. "Now you're ready."

I fingered my mother's ruby and diamond necklace that my dad had given me. I wished my mom was alive and here to see me now.

"She is." Dad's voice peppered the air.

I tore my gaze away from my reflection to find him waltzing in, dressed in a tuxedo with a red bow tie. His hair was pulled back and secured at the nape of his neck, his face was smooth, and his green eyes were cloudy as he came up behind me.

"Your mom is watching down on you." He grasped my shoulders gently and guided me around. "And if she was here, she would say how beautiful her daughter is and how proud she is of you. Just like I am. I can never take back that I left you with your aunt when I was deployed overseas or that you ended up in foster care. But I want you to know that I've loved you since the day your mom told me she was pregnant with you and Sam." He leaned in to kiss me on the forehead. "You've had a rough life, but now I want you to live like you've never lived before."

Tears welled up. I blinked several times, trying not to let any spill, or else my makeup would be ruined. Then again, it didn't matter. I was probably going to be crying all day.

"I love you, Dad."

"One thing before we go. I know things have been crazy, and you've been planning your wedding, but I'm not sure if you remember. You and Sam had a birthday last week. I completely forgot about it with all the cleanup we've been doing. But you both officially turned eighteen."

Holy cow! "I did forget, but we did have other things to worry about."

"I thought your birthday was in February," Darcy said.

I forgot I hadn't explained to Darcy why we had a birthday in December and not February like Sam and I had thought and had always celebrated. "The short version is because Sam and I were born with the natural-born vampire gene, and our birth records had to be changed to reflect a normal human blood type. Otherwise, our DNA would be in question, and that would raise a lot of red flags within the human government. In fact, our birth dates are changed as well to further conceal our true identity from humans."

"Well, birthdays are fun," she said. "But a wedding beats a birthday. We can celebrate another time."

Agreed. I might have been eighteen, but I felt so much older after how my body had changed when I turned vampire, not to mention all the fighting and training and stress I'd been through.

"Darcy's right," Dad said. "Today is by far a huge celebration. You've turned into a wonderful young lady. And I couldn't be more proud."

"You're not helping my tears." I caught one before it slid down my cheek.

Dad held out his elbow. "Shall we?"

"Can I have a minute?"

"We'll be in the hall," Dad said as he escorted Darcy out with him.

I kept blinking until my eyes dried, although the butterflies were having a party in my stomach. I was about to get married to one of the most gorgeous vampires a girl could want. Dad was right. I had had a rough life. So much had happened. Dad had all but disappeared on Sam and me when we could barely walk. Our mother had died at a young age. Sam and I had jumped from one foster family to another until the day our last foster dad had attacked me. Since that day, my life had changed so drastically. But in the end, I wouldn't have changed a moment, day, or anything, although I could've done without Edmund and his team. Still, if it weren't for him, I might not have been getting married.

And on that note, I walked out to start my new life.

22

———

WEBB

As I fidgeted with the bow tie on my tuxedo, I couldn't believe that I was actually standing in a bedroom in Victor Costner's mansion, waiting to get married. In mere minutes, I would say I do to the most beautiful creature I'd ever laid eyes on.

I'd barely seen Jo since we had returned from Alaska, and I'd been having withdrawals. Every time I'd made a point of seeking her out during the last four weeks, she was doing something for the wedding, which was probably a good thing since I had business to shore up before I retired. The elders had approved my retirement papers, and I couldn't have been more stoked.

Speaking of the elders, Dyson had been shipped off to the vampire prison in Puerto Rico, which left an opening for a new elder. Hollings and Radisson made an offer to Steven, who had gladly accepted. So that left Steven's position open. He had asked if I would reconsider retiring to take on the role of commander, but I'd said no thank you. I was done with the military, and if I did want to work at some point in the future, then I would do something along the lines of private security or private detective work. For now, work wasn't on my agenda. My final responsibilities before my wedding day had been making arrangements to move Nicki to the same vampire prison as Dyson then working with Sam to erase Agent Thomas and Dr. Case's memories. Steven and I had decided to wipe Case's memories rather than stick him in a prison somewhere. He knew too much. Even part of Nicki's memories had been wiped. We couldn't risk an ounce of what Patrick had concocted getting into anyone's hands, whether human or vampire.

In fact, Steven had had a team of folks clean out an office complex that Patrick had owned. Jonah had gotten the key that helped us to confiscate all Patrick's research data. Dr. Vieira had wanted to examine it, but Steven had said no. Instead, the servers and all Patrick's notebooks and files were burned.

Footsteps clobbered on the wood floor outside the door before Tripp entered, looking as though he'd just stepped off the pages of a GQ magazine. His tuxedo was sculpted to his broad body, his blond locks were slicked back but free about his shoulders, and his jaw was clean-shaven. "Ready?"

Even though nerves poked at my stomach, I was more than ready. I couldn't wait to see my bride, kiss my bride, say I do, and above all else, make love to my vampire beauty. I blew by Tripp and out the door into the short hall.

"Wait up." He chuckled. "We're not putting out a fire."

"You don't understand." I stopped in the doorway of the large room on the first floor of the mansion, the same room in which the charity event had been held many months ago.

Soft music played in the distance.

Tripp clapped me on the shoulder. "Oh, I understand. Let's not forget you've been talking about your big night with Jo since you proposed to her. My only advice—go slow and be gentle."

I angled my head even though I knew he was talking about how I had wanted to make love to her since I met her. I'd confided in my best friend from the beginning. "I'm always gentle."

He laughed, showing white teeth. "You may be, but your body will be screaming."

No doubt about that. "Well, I have to get married first."

We walked into the pine-scented room that was saturated with big and small Christmas trees, poinsettias, chairs filled with guests, and a piano. We hadn't invited many people. We'd wanted to keep it small and relegated to family and close friends.

George nodded at me from the front row, while Sam, Kraft, and Kodiak strutted down from the back of the room, dressed in tuxedos to match Tripp and me. All three were groomsmen.

Kraft's mahogany gaze swept over me. "Are you ready?"

"You better treat my sister well," Sam said.

Kodiak rolled his eyes at Sam. "Seriously, dude? Webb is the most put-together man I know. It's Jo who better treat Webb well."

I chuckled. "Okay, you two. No fighting. Jo would tear us a new one if any of our tuxedos got ripped before the vows."

Laughter rolled off them.

Victor crossed the room over to us. His dark hair was slicked back, and a black robe covered his suit. "In your places as we rehearsed last night."

Victor had been appointed by the council of elders to marry us. Unlike the human world, vampires didn't need a priest or a minister, nor did the person marrying a couple need to be licensed. He just needed approval from the council of elders. Victor had asked Jo and me if he could marry us. He'd wanted to repay us in some way for saving his grandson, even though opening up his home was payment enough, at least in my book.

Once everyone was in place—Tripp next to me, then Sam, Kraft, and Kodiak—and the guests were settled, Matthew keyed up the piano. On the first key, Abbey came into view from around chairs in the back row. She wore a white dress and black shoes with white lace ankle socks. She smiled and waved before Alia, who was behind her, urged Abbey to throw rose petals down before she took a step. All eyes watched the little girl as I kept searching behind Alia, Crysta, Olivia, and Darcy for Jo.

Once Abbey reached the end of the aisle near me, she ran up and hugged my leg. That wasn't in the rehearsal, but who cared?

I squatted down while the bridesmaids slowly closed the distance to the makeshift altar. "You look beautiful."

She shied away.

"Why don't you go sit with George," I said.

Abbey beamed up at me. "When am I going to live with you and Jo?"

"Not for a few weeks. We talked about this, remember?"

Her mom, Rachel, didn't have any family. Rachel's mom had passed away after battling cancer for years, her father had died in a car wreck, and Rachel didn't have any siblings. Even if she did have family, I wasn't sure if we would have allowed Abbey to live with humans, considering her supernatural powers and the fact that she was naturally turning into a vampire.

Steven and I had talked about asking Alia to take care of Abbey, but Jo wouldn't hear of it. She wanted Abbey to live with us, and I agreed. Since Jo couldn't have kids, Abbey would be the perfect addition to our family. Regardless, Jo and I did want a few weeks alone to spend some quality time together before Abbey joined us.

She nodded, biting her lip, almost as though she was going to cry.

"What's wrong?" If she was about to have a vision, I might lose it unless her vision was of something happy.

She threw her tiny arms around me. "I love you."

I kissed her on the cheek. "I love you too."

She squeezed me tightly then darted over to sit with George.

By the time I stood up, all the bridesmaids were next to me, and the music had stopped. The guests rose, fabric rustling, whispers buzzing, as all eyes went to Jo and her father. My heart stopped when my gaze landed on Jo. From there, I didn't see anything or anyone else. All sounds died. My knees even buckled.

Tripp caught my arm. "I got you."

Jo's lips tipped up in a generous smile as she clutched her father, who I would guess was holding her steady because I could hear her heart ramming against her ribs. Hell, my pulse was doing the same. Ever so slowly, her father guided her down the aisle toward me. The closer she got, the more I itched to touch her soft skin, feel her lips on mine, and breathe in her lavender scent.

Once she reached me, Steven lifted her veil, kissed her on both cheeks, then grasped her hand and placed it in mine. "Webb London, I expect nothing but the best for my daughter."

I nodded because it was the only thing I could do. I was afraid that if I spoke, only a squeak would come out. I took Jo's cold, trembling hand, and we locked eyes for a moment before facing Victor.

He started in on a speech about vampire laws and marriage. I tuned him out. All I could do was stare at how Jo's gown clung to her curves, savor how sweet she smelled, and marvel at how my heart soared with happiness because I had finally found someone as beautiful as her to spend eternity with.

23

___

JO

No sooner had Webb and I checked into the Waldorf Hotel—the same one we'd stayed in last month—than my palms began to sweat. My body had been iced up until now, simply from nerves. In fact, the entire ceremony was a blur. All I kept thinking about was our future and waking up to Webb every morning. I also thought about what we would do with our time now that we would be Abbey's adoptive parents.

First and foremost, Webb and I would love her unconditionally, and as she grew, we would teach her how to handle her powers and help her as she naturally transitioned into a vampire.

The door to our suite closed with a bang, jarring me from my haze. Webb had stepped out to get some ice, and now he was back.

He set down the ice bucket on the bar near the bottle of champagne. "You haven't moved from that spot."

The suite was different from the one Webb and I had stayed in. This one was larger, had a gas fireplace, and the atmosphere felt cozier and warmer. I needed warmth, although sizing up Webb was sending heat all over my body in a frenzied way.

He'd lost the tuxedo jacket, bow tie, and shoes. I raised an

185

eyebrow at my husband. *Eeek.* It felt weird to say *husband*. Still, I hadn't seen him take off his jacket, let alone his shoes. Maybe I shouldn't have been staring out at Boston's night skyline.

Webb sauntered up to me, his shoulder-length hair flowing free about his shoulders. He hadn't pulled it back for the wedding either, which was fine with me since he looked sexier with his hair down.

He gently grasped the sides of my arms and guided me around so I was again looking out at Boston. Then he slowly unzipped my dress, the sound spiking my adrenaline.

I glanced at our reflection in the window. His blue eyes were like headlights until they began to shift to vampire black. Then, ever so slowly, his fangs lowered, and my belly did a wild dance. This was really happening. I'd wanted him desperately for so long, and now that we were married… *Yikes.* We were married. I was married. He was my husband.

He lowered his head, and his hot breath tickled my neck, making the goose bumps flare to life. "Your heartbeat is off the charts, angel. Breathe. We don't have to do anything if you're not ready."

My dress slid to the floor, exposing my bra and panties. I was more than ready to seal our relationship, our marriage, but I'd never had sex before. *Will I be any good? Will I feel pain?* When I was human and attended high school, I'd overheard girls talking about their first times and how painful they had been. *You've endured stabbings. The pain from sex can't be as bad.*

Webb's fangs grazed my neck. "I promise I'll be gentle."

I sank back against him as his hands roamed lazily over my stomach. "I know. It's just I've wanted you for so long, but I've never done this before."

He guided me to face him, his eyelids heavy as he kissed me on my forehead, then on my eyelids, my cheeks, my neck, my ears, and everywhere but my lips. My body tingled as my limbs went languid. I arched backward and angled my neck, wanting him to sink his fangs into me and feel the tingling sensation that overpowered my body when he sucked my blood into his mouth.

His large hand caressed one breast then the other.

I moaned. He growled. Then he guided me back until my body was against the window. The cold pane did nothing to quench the heat building inside me.

Slowly, steadily, and with calculated precision, he lifted one of my arms over my head then the other before he levered back. "Don't move." The command in his words made me shiver in delight.

Even more trembles of excitement went through me when his hooded gaze swept over every inch of my body as though he was mapping the spots he wanted to attack first.

"Webb." I said his name, but I swore the girl against the window wasn't me.

He unbuttoned his shirt as he kept his gaze glued to mine. Then, before I could track another of his movements, the shirt went sailing across the room.

I swallowed thickly, licking my lips. The man was built to perfection. He stood within an arm's reach with packed abs, a broad chest, and strong muscled arms that I wanted around me. I itched to touch him and jump into his arms.

As though he knew my thought, his husky voice peppered the air. "Don't move, angel."

I pouted. "Why not?"

He grinned, a slow and sexy smile that promised a night of pure pleasure. "Because I want to kiss you everywhere." He closed the distance between us and kneeled down before his calloused hands went to the backs of my thighs. Then he pressed soft lips to one thigh then the other before he kissed his way up my body, his fangs grazing, tickling, and eliciting tingles and all kinds of other sensations.

I drove my fingers through his hair, pulling and tugging. Then, before I could take a breath, I was in his arms. At first, I thought he would head for the bedroom, but instead, he settled on a furry carpet in front of the fireplace then set me down on two feet. The flame flickered, highlighting the sharp angles of his jaw, his full lips, and those cobalt-blue eyes that seemed to pierce right through me.

He reached around my head and pulled out my clip, sending my hair tumbling down around me. "You're stunning."

I gnawed my lip as I looked away. He'd told me many times how beautiful I was, but at that moment, standing in nothing more than a bra and panties, I felt a little shy.

His powerful hands flattened on my cheeks. "My vows were pure, angel. I will be gentle. I will treat you like an equal. I will cherish you. I will love you unconditionally and for eternity. And above all else, I am yours until the day I die."

I'd cried at the altar when he'd said his vows. He'd had nothing but love in his eyes, and he'd spoken with such conviction that he had many of the guests sniffling. But now I smiled so wide that my face hurt as the nerves swirling around inside me waned. "You will always have my soul."

He struck quickly, his fangs sinking into my neck. I cried out, or more like moaned loudly, the feeling euphoric as his emotions blended with mine. The mind-blocking potion had worn off. So it was easy to get inside his head. Images of him and me rolling around on the carpet beneath us flickered in his mind. I snaked my hands around his waist to his back and pressed my fingers into his heated skin.

He let out a groan as he retracted his fangs, licking the puncture wounds as he expertly removed my bra. Then, without warning, I was on my back, and he was hovering over me. He lowered his head to capture a nipple between his lips. I fisted the carpet in both hands, arching into him as he moved to my other breast, his hair caressing my skin.

I trembled and squirmed, enjoying how his tongue swirled as he sucked, his canines poking lightly. All of it was too much yet not enough. I wanted more of him, naked.

I slipped my hands in between us and reached for his belt. But before I could unbuckle it, he was on his feet, shucking the rest of his clothes.

I held back a gasp at the sight of him. If I'd thought his chest was God-like, I was wrong. My gaze traveled down his body, mapping every part of him right down to his groin. My cheeks flushed, and I almost looked away, but I couldn't. My breathing grew shallow, and all I could think about was him inside me.

He dropped to his knees and with gentle fingers removed my panties. I watched in quiet fascination as he sucked in a sharp breath, while I lay bare, mind, body, and soul. I wanted him in my head. I wanted him to see what I was thinking, how I felt, and what I wanted him to do to me.

"I know what you want," he said, his deep, husky voice sliding over my skin like a bath of warm chocolate.

I held my lip hostage. "You know what I'm thinking?"

He nodded as his hands roamed over my entire body, sending flares of heat everywhere. "I drank your blood. You're a little timid, yet you want me to make love to you so badly that it hurts."

My gaze fell to his groin, which was hard and ready.

He positioned himself over me, his hands on either side of my head. We locked eyes as he slowly entered me.

I stilled at the tightness and dull pain.

He leaned down, brushing my lips with his. His long locks fell forward to create a curtain around us. "Bring your knees up. It will help."

I did as he said, and he inched in more. I winced, taking in a deep breath. When I did, he pushed in all the way then stopped.

I dug my nails into his back as a wave of pain hit me. But as he moved in then out in an extremely slow fashion, the pain subsided, and my muscles began to loosen.

A satisfied grin emerged on his face as his eyes drifted close, his body moving against mine. "I love you more than you know."

At that moment, with him inside me, my body burned for more

than making love. I had to taste him. I pulled him down then sank my fangs into his neck. He rolled us without breaking our connection. Now I was on top, and his hands were shaping my hips, helping me move with him while I swallowed the sweet nectar coating my throat as stars began to burst.

Webb let out a low growl as we tumbled again until he was on top. I broke free from his neck and found that his eyes were wild as though a predator had overtaken the man. The air crackled around us, or maybe it was the fire. Our emotions mingled and swirled as he moved faster, taking me higher and higher. That pain I'd felt at first was a distant memory. All I could feel now was love, ecstasy, and the sensation that I was about to explode, a feeling I'd never experienced before. Just as I reached a jumping-off point, Webb stopped. Sweat dripped off him and onto me.

Before I could protest, he popped to his feet, bringing me upright with him. He grasped my hand and tugged me into the bedroom.

My eyes went wide. "When did you do this?" Rose petals covered the bed, tons of flowers graced the dresser, the scent of lilies stood out above all, and candlelight flickered around the room. I went over to the bed and picked up a handful of petals, soft and silky.

Webb's woodsy scent announced his closeness before his body was flush against my backside. His hands came around to my stomach, and his lips settled on that sensitive spot behind my ear. "You deserve more than this."

I turned in his arms to find the vampire completely mesmerized. I didn't have to ask him why. A simple touch of his hot skin, and I was in his head, seeing every image he wanted me to see. He took me on a walk down memory lane when he'd first laid eyes on me in Principal Jackson's office at the human high school. He'd never banked on how beautiful I would be. He'd thought that I would be ordinary.

I angled my head. "Ordinary?" We shouldn't have been talking, especially when his hardness was poking against me. But I had to know.

"You don't blend in with a crowd, angel. You sucked me in when I looked into those silver eyes of yours. It was that day I knew I would marry you."

My hands coasted up his arms. "So you married me," I teased. "Now what?"

He guided me backward. When my legs hit the bed, all I could do was sit. He trapped me in between his arms as he pressed his hands on either side of me on the bed. Then he licked the seam of my lips, begging for access. Instead of opening for him, I scooted to the middle of the bed, the rose petals soft against my bare skin. He followed me like a true predator, crawling slowly as though he was ready to pounce, and I had no doubt he was ready.

Butterflies winged through my stomach as he sucked one nipple into his mouth.

"You taste sweeter than ever." His voice was husky, his touch electric.

Sparks of ecstasy popped in the air until he entered me. Then an inferno took shape when I clenched around him. All of a sudden, his hands were on my butt, pulling me to him as though I wasn't close enough. My belly spun into a web of tingles that tightened each time I met his thrust. Then his pace picked up, his hands clenching my hips, our eyes locked together, our hearts beating as one, our breathing shallow, our minds in sync. The world around me disappeared. The earth could shatter, and as long as I was with Webb, I didn't care if the hotel burned down. I was right where I belonged.

Sweat coated our bodies, making our union slick. He slowed his pace before sliding his fingers between us to settle on my tiny bundle of nerves. I swallowed thickly when he moved his finger around once then twice before a million stars burst behind my eyelids. I rode out the explosion that took place inside me as he pummeled into me hard and fast, grunting and groaning until his mouth crashed into mine, pushing his tongue in, taking everything he could. Gone was the gentle vampire. In his place was a man on a mission, who wanted nothing more than to love the woman of his dreams—the woman he wanted for eternity. Our bodies glided against each other. Then he broke the kiss and roared my name, his body shaking, his chest heaving. It was a beautiful sight to see how I affected him.

He rolled off me then tugged me into his arms so that we were facing each other. "Are you all right?" His breathing slowed.

I buried my face against his chest. "More than all right. You?"

"Perfect, angel."

It was perfect. I would've never imagined that my life would turn out this way—married to a vampire, a gorgeous man with a bright future that involved a little girl who would be our daughter. Even though I was only eighteen, I wouldn't trade one moment of what had happened for anything else in the world.

Webb's heart thumped in my ear. "Words can't describe how much I love you."

I'd lost my humanity because he was my destiny, and even though we had flitted on the edge of misery for a brief time, we had an eternity to show each other that our love was infinite.

On that note, I lifted up and kissed him like I'd never kissed him before. I nipped, bit, took, tasted, and got lost in him, in us, and in the perfect future ahead of us.

GLOSSARY OF TERMS

Natural-born vampire: A human born with the vampire gene that, when activated, will turn them into a vampire.

Activation process: Those who carry the vampire gene can only turn by drinking the blood of their vampire father at the age of sixteen years or older.

Council of Elders – A group of five vampires who set the laws.

Genetic engineering: Turning humans into vampires through a process of restructuring their DNA.

Cobalt – A vampire's kryptonite. The metal will kill a vampire if staked through the heart. It will also burn a vampire's skin if they come in contact with it.

Reproduction: A natural-born vampire is born by a male vampire and a human female with a rare blood type of Vel negative.

Council of Eternal Affairs: The legal department of the vampire government.

Vampire characteristics: Sunlight doesn't burn them. Their hearts beat at <5 bpm. Skin temperature is ten degrees cooler than a human. Eye color changes to black except for a few chosen ones.

Steven Mason: Vampire and father to twins Jo and Sam Mason. He's dubbed the most powerful of all vampires because of his many powers, including his mind-reading abilities. He can only read minds when touching someone except when it comes to his children. His normal eye color is green. His vampire eye color is silver.

Jo Mason: Turned at sixteen. Powers include seeing the future through her dreams, mind-reading without touching a person, telekinesis, and she's an elemental with the ability to manipulate water, air, earth, and fire. Her normal eye color is silver. Her vampire eye color is violet.

Sam Mason: Turned at sixteen. Powers include feeling what others feel (Empath), telekinesis, and he can compel a person using a series of numbers woven into a magical spell. He's also an elemental with the ability to manipulate water, air, earth, and fire. His normal eye color is green. His vampire eye color is silver.

Jupiter Sentinels: A secret and elite Navy SEAL Team within the military. Their role is to help the human military and guard the supernatural world.

Plutariums: A rogue team of vampires who want power and to engineer an army that would change humans into vampires.

Guardians: Vampires who are equivalent to the human police.

ABOUT THE AUTHOR

Bestselling author **S.B. Alexander** is an independent author with over 20 titles to date. She writes paranormal, new adult, and sweet romances that feature hot heroes stealing hearts.

S.B. or Susan as she likes to be called is a navy veteran, former high school teacher, and former corporate sales executive. She's a lover of sports, especially baseball, although nowadays you can find her glued to the TV during football season.

When she's not writing, she's a full-time caregiver to her soul mate of twenty-three years who got a bad deal in life when he was diagnosed with ALS. Her motto: "Life is too short to waste. So live every moment like it's your last."

You can connect with S.B. Alexander in the following ways:
Reader Group: https://sbalexander.com/beastsandbitches
Author Website: https://sbalexander.com
Newsletter: https://sbalexander.com/newsletter
Email: susan@sbalexander.com

NEVER MISS A NEW RELEASE:
Sign up for her Author App
iTunes: https://bit.ly/sbalexanderitunes
Android: https://bit.ly/sbalexanderandroid

facebook.com/sbalexander.authorpage

twitter.com/sbalex_author

instagram.com/sbalexanderauthor

bookbub.com/authors/s-b-alexander

goodreads.com/sbalexander

amazon.com/author/sbalexander

ALSO BY S.B. ALEXANDER

MAXWELL SERIES

Upper Young Adult/New Adult Contemporary Romance

Dare to Kiss

Dare to Dream

Dare to Love

Dare to Dance

Dare to Live

Dare to Breathe

Dare to Embrace

THE MAXWELL FAMILY SAGA SERIES

Young Adult Sweet Romance

My Heart to Touch

My Heart to Hold

My Heart to Give

My Heart to Keep

THE VAMPIRE NAVY SEAL SERIES

Paranormal Romance

On the Edge of Humanity

On the Edge of Eternity

On the Edge of Destiny

On the Edge of Misery

Visit https://sbalexander.com/all-books/ to learn more about S.B. Alexander books and future releases. Please note release dates are subject to change based on reader demand and the author's schedule. Subscribing to the author's newsletter or following her on Facebook is the best way to stay updated with planned new releases.